Wiseguys in Paradise

A NOVEL

Stephen Spotte

Published by Open Books

I told lies and wondered where I would go if my own
past was all I had left.

— James Ellroy, *The Black Dahlia*

Introduction

———◆◆———

THIS NOVEL COMPRISES A narrative and characters that arose entirely from my imagination and are not intended to resemble actual events or specific persons, living or dead. Coney Island in Brooklyn, New York, and Key West in the Florida Keys are real, of course. Some of the places mentioned at those locations existed at one time, and a few still do, although my treatment of them is entirely fictitious.

I lived and worked for a time in Coney Island in the early 1970s and know it well. I also once lived in the Florida Keys, and in April 2007 my two best friends and I held a last hurrah at the legendary Atlantic Shores Resort in Key West where for a week we raised hell. A month later the place was razed, and a modern hotel now stands in its place. I call my fictional reincarnation the Ocean Shores Resort. One of those buddies died in July the same year, the other in February of the next. The tale of our venture there is told in my memoir *The Smoking Horse: A Memoir in Pieces*.

The original Atlantic Shores Resort was world-famous and remains the subject of lively memories posted on the Internet. My fictitious Catalano's Ristorante bears a vague resemblance to the renowned Gargiulo's, a Coney Island landmark on West 15th Street since 1907. When I frequented the place it was staffed by ancient and rude Italian waiters who never smiled and behaved as if we drinkers and diners posed a major annoyance. But the food was terrific and well worth suffering their disdain.

Graham Greene once described certain of his novels as "little entertainments." Consider this one of mine.

Stephen Spotte
Longboat Key, Florida
August 2023

Chapter 1

————◆◆————

IT WAS SEPTEMBER 1959. I was twenty-one, twenty-two, something like that. I don't remember exactly. Birthdays weren't celebrated in my family, and as I got older it seemed stupid to celebrate them alone, so I basically stopped thinking about them. A birthday was just another day, nothing special. I admit that going to birthday parties for other kids and never to my own was a little weird. While their moms hovered around asking if we wanted more cake or ice cream I pictured my own mom on the couch in her nightgown listening to the radio or watching TV, waiting for my dad to come home so she could tear into him about how shitty her life was. She usually had a drink in one hand and a cigarette in the other and was too sloshed to make supper.

I'd just mustered out of the Army after serving a two-year hitch, all of it spent in the States. After basic training I was sent to Fort Lee, Virginia, for thirteen weeks to complete Advanced Individual Training for my military 63B MOS, which was Light Wheel Mechanics. In English, the Army trained me to fix vehicles that rolled on wheels, as opposed to crawling on tracks, an upgrade to the auto mechanics classes from high school. Afterward, I was transferred to Fort Dix in New Jersey and spent the remainder of my hitch there. Not exactly exciting, but not dangerous either. What the hell, it was a job and experience for being a civilian mechanic.

There was another guy in the program, a Puerto Rican from New York named Roberto, and we sort of became friends and hung out sometimes when off duty. During a smoke break he told me his uncle owned a busy garage in Coney Island in Brooklyn and that he had a job waiting when he got out. He and the uncle talked on the phone fairly often, and his uncle said he could take me on too if I wanted to stay in the area instead of going home. Roberto was scheduled to be discharged a couple of months before me. He wrote his uncle's number on a piece of paper, and I stuck it in my wallet.

When my discharge rolled around I thought, why go home? I knew what was waiting. Risking my life doing shift work in the coal mines or sweating topside at a hardscrabble garage busting knuckles on the junkers broke miners dragged in and wanted fixed on the cheap.

I was an only child. Maybe I should say an invisible child, the desire to be inconspicuous resulting from my home life. I worked hard at trying to vanish into the background, driven by two motivating factors: a

dysfunctional family and a debilitating speech imped-
iment that rendered me self-conscious to the extent
of feeling like a freak. I'll say more about that later.
To call me an unhappy kid by any definition wouldn't
do the label justice. In our family we had only ourselves: no aunts and uncles, no cousins. All four of my
grandparents had died before I was born. Nothing
remained of them but a half-dozen sepia photos in
dusty frames hanging on the walls. The faces looking
out were dull and unsmiling, projecting an aura of
sadness and dissatisfaction.

Mom wasn't good at domestic responsibilities. She
didn't clean house, except now and then to empty her
ashtray she kept on the coffee table in front of the TV.
Dirty dishes were left in the sink. Sometimes when
Pa came home from the mines covered in black dust
and dragging his ass he might wash them and stick
them in the drainboard. Grocery shop? Mom didn't
do much of that either. If she made it to the company
store it was to replenish her bourbon supply. While
there she might pick up a couple of items, notably
junk food, unless even that was inconvenient because
her soaps were starting. Prepare meals? We were on
our own, pretty much.

No one bothered to wake me for school, so early
on I started doing it myself, taking the alarm clock
Mom should have been using. Often as not, hunger
woke me before it rang. Then I brushed my teeth like
a good little boy, dressed, and went to the kitchen to
forage for breakfast. I'd climb onto the counter and
look in the cupboards for cereal. Next, I opened the
fridge checking for milk, bread, butter, jam—anything.

Sometimes I got lucky, but often breakfast was a few handfuls of dry cornflakes or nothing at all if the cereal and bread were gone. Meanwhile, Mom would be passed out on the couch snoring like a rhinoceros. If Pa worked second shift he would already be gone, if first shift, he would just be leaving work and heading home. I had no way of knowing, so it was off to catch the school bus. Lunch? None.

Among other delusions, Mom had this notion that life was passing her by, that she wasn't catching any breaks and this was everyone's fault but hers. What she needed, she reminded Pa and me often enough, was a change of scenery. She was too classy to waste away in a coal camp. She wanted to move to Louis-ville or Richmond where she could dress nicely in the latest fashions, go out to dinner and be seen, and live in a beautiful house with a maid and a gardener and maybe even a chauffeur. "Well?" she'd say to Pa from the couch. "Are you listening to me, goddammit?"

"I hear you," he'd say. "And just what would we do for money in these places?"

"You'd work."

"At what? I'm a coal miner."

"You could quit and do something else."

"That's all I know. Plus, I'm vested in the retirement plan, and we'd be throwing hit away. We ain't moving, so git over hit and quit drinking so much. Hit makes you mean and lazy."

Then Mom would go into a tizzy, shouting and waving her glass and cigarette around, spittle flying out of her mouth. After a while she'd shout herself out and go into a coughing fit, hawking up big yellow gobs. But it wasn't over because she'd start in on Pa about something else, such as forgetting to refill the ice trays when she was the one who forgot. Pa drank only beer and never used ice cubes. As I grew older I'd often take the brunt of her anger and disappointment over having to drink her liquor warm, although I never used ice cubes either. When one of these scenes started I'd step outside and walk around, even in the rain or snow, or go to my room and shut the door. I couldn't wait to be old enough to leave home.

———————

Before disappearing into the civilian population Roberto had mentioned his cousin Angel who worked at a famous Sicilian restaurant in Coney Island. It operated as one of those rare fire-free zones where the New York Mafia families were safe from one another, and anybody from a *capo* to a wiseguy could eat a meal in peace without having to sit with his back pressed against the wall. Roberto said if I couldn't reach his uncle once I was a civilian that Angel would know how to get in touch. He wrote down the number of the restaurant, and I stuck it in my wallet with the other one.

Maybe it was fate, but when I tried phoning the garage the day before being discharged a recording told me the number was no longer in service. Did Roberto screw up? Who knows. I threw away that piece of paper and called the restaurant. Someone with an accent answered, "*Ciao*, Catalano's." I asked for Angel. The voice replied *un momento* and shouted to someone in what probably was Italian. After a couple of minutes a different voice picked up and said, "*Este es Angel.*" He pronounced it Awn-HEL. I said my name and mentioned Roberto. "Aw yeah, he said youse might phone. Call me Angel, like, wit wings." I explained how I didn't have Roberto's number, his personal one.

"That's 'cause Robbie ain't never had a phone," Angel said. "Come over to the restaurant. It's Catalano's in Coney Island at the ass-end of Brooklyn. The D train stops at the aquarium. The stop officially is Boardwalk and West Eighth Street. Catalano's is a coupla blocks west on Surf Avenue. Need directions, ast anybody. The place has been around forever. I'm here till late."

A bunch of guys from the base were getting off the bus in Manhattan, some on leave, others newly discharged like me and heading for other parts of the country. By luck, I sat beside a guy visiting his parents in Brooklyn for the weekend. We dived into the subway and jumped on the F train together, and he said to switch to the D train at Sheepshead Bay.

I found Catalano's and told the doorman I was there to see Angel. He yelled in Italian through the open door, and eventually a skinny guy with long greasy hair appeared from somewhere in back. He was wearing a dirty white apron and heavy rubber gloves up to his elbows. I said who I was and we shook. His hand felt like one of those bathtub toys. "Sorry," he said. "I sometimes forget I'm wearing these fucking things. Follow me."

There were two swinging doors to the kitchen marked *Entrada* and *Uscita* so the waiters and bussers didn't bump into each other coming and going. Angel explained this as we entered the kitchen. "A joke," he said over his shoulder, "is that an 'Irish exit' is to leave a party witout telling nobody. An 'Italian exit' is to leave holding a vermouth cocktail. The wops think that's funny as hell. Go figure."

Two short guys looking like Mayan statues were standing side by side at a double sink scrubbing big metal pots. Angel said something to them in Spanish, which they obviously heard but didn't acknowledge. Nearby, a commercial dishwasher gurgled and sluiced.

A toothpick disguised as a scarecrow shuffled in. His threadbare tux probably fit him forty years ago but now was several sizes too big. He was bald with a pale crepey face and moved with an air of ownership. Angel leaned against the counter and announced, "Hey, the big boss is here. This is Giovanni, which in Sicilian means 'gift from God,' but I call him Hercules on account of he's built like Charlie Atlas."

The man stopped and glared at Angel, who said, "Got a new victim for the kitchen crew." He jerked his thumb in my direction. "Hercules is the head waiter, the main cheese, the big casino, the chief honcho, *il grande capo della cucina*. Hey, Hercules, how long youse been in America?" This evidently was a standard routine for the two of them, like Abbot and Costello's Who's on First.

The guy continued glaring at Angel as if looks were lethal. "Fifty-two year I been in America, and fifty-two year inna this restaurant. I starta working the next day I arrive when I am eleven year. I starta with the mop inna my hand, and I worka day and night, no time for school, my family, we needa the money. You spics, you never grateful, always complain, never, how you say, satisfied. You don't give no respect to nobody."

"Like the wiseguys who kill time in this place?"

"They deserva respect too. Everybody deserva respect. Ah." He dismissed us with a wave and turned his back. Just then a waiter came through the door and Giovanni started gesturing and yelling at him in Italian.

I asked Angel what was happening. "The waiter came through the wrong door, a definite no-no in the restaurant business. Hercules is ripping him a new one, telling him, 'Hey, stupid shit, youse been here forty years and still don't know the right hand from the left?' It's typical greaseball stuff. You get usta it."

I told Angel I didn't need a kitchen job, that I was hoping to get in touch with Roberto's uncle.

"It don't matter. Showing up here gets youse a free Italian dinner and then youse can leave if youse want, but I gotta say, Robbie's uncle currently resides in the slammer. That busy garage he ran was actually a busy chop-shop. All the merchandise was hot. I ain't heard from Robbie since, hell, I can't remember. He could be in San Juan for all I know. Point is, there ain't no job. Sit at that little break table in the corner, and I'll get youse some chow."

He went into the restaurant and returned with a bottle of red wine and a glass. The bottle had been opened but was nearly full. As he poured he said, "Some wine snob sent it back, like, what the fuck, this is Florence or something. It's table wine, for chrissakes. Vintage? There ain't any." Then he walked the several steps to where the chefs were hustling and brought a salad with vinaigrette dressing, a basket of crusty bread, and a pile of veal ravioli in spicy marinara sauce. I hadn't eaten all day, and everything tasted terrific. "Let's sit outside," he said when I'd finished. He grabbed a clean wine glass for himself off the rack and we went out to the alley. It stank of rotting garbage and piss evaporating off ancient concrete. He was holding the glasses and bottle and directed me to pull two wine crates out of the dumpster to sit on. We got comfortable. He produced a pack of cigarettes and shook up a couple. "Smoke?"

"Thanks," I said, "I'm out."

He lit us up, then shook up a third and slid it gently behind my ear. "For later," he said.

"I reckon I'll take the job."

"Good, 'cause I already told the bookkeeper to put youse on the payroll as of today. Youse can sign her papers tomorrow. The kitchen crew starts at eleven in time for the lunch hour. Lunch goes on through the afternoon. It's a big deal to the dagos. They like to eat heavy in mid-afternoon. Youse can crash at my place tonight. I got a room wit two beds in a fleabag hotel around the corner. If youse stick around we split the rent. The manager, Manny, is Puerto Rican, so on payday—that's every Friday—youse give me eight bucks for the coming week, and I pass it along to him. Gotta warn youse, no room service unless youse count junkie hookers pounding on the door in the middle of the night." He laughed and topped up our glasses. "Where youse from?"

"West Virginia."

"I figured somewhere in stump-jump country. The accent." I nodded.

"Well, let's toss these off and get to work. Our two

amigos from Central America been toting the whole bale by theirself and deserve a break. I'll introduce youse, but *ellos no hablan ingles*. They'll say, *'mucho gusto,'* which means, 'nice to meet youse,' and hold out a limp hand. They're honest dudes, and they bust ass, but real shy, probably 'cause they're illegal. Don't be surprised if them's the last words they ever speak to youse."

I got in the groove pretty fast. There isn't much new to learn about washing dishes, and it's not like this was my first gig on a kitchen cleanup crew. Angel showed me how to load the dishwasher and advised soaking the pots several minutes in heavy detergent when they came from the chefs. It loosens the pasta stuck to the sides, which makes scrubbing them easier. Otherwise, it was just dishwashing. Some days and nights were busy, others slow.

September and most of October had slipped past. We were putting in twelve-hours shifts with time-and-a-half for anything over eight hours, so the pay was actually pretty decent, and the food was great. I never bought food except morning coffee and a donut or bagel. Lunch and dinner were covered by the restaurant.

Catalano's closed Mondays when the staff got some time off. I was using those days to walk around and familiarize myself with Coney Island, which served as its own perpetual freak show open 24/7. The New York Aquarium was near the subway stop, and one day I paid admission to see the exhibits and whale show. The whales looked like gigantic white marshmallows, and I never had suspected that fish come in so many shapes and colors. The place was amazing.

I was peacefully watching the fish that day when a commotion broke out. The public area was dark except for footlights and what light streamed out from the aquariums. I glanced around and saw a couple of cops I recognized from the 60th precinct, guys of Italian heritage who sometimes dropped in at Catalano's while on patrol for a snort or two on the house. They were frog-marching a short guy toward the exit. I learned later that he was famous for hiding in the crowd and feeling up the women, harmless but a nuisance. He owned a season's pass, but often disguised himself to get past the ticket takers.

Angel had a girlfriend, a waitress at a diner out on Flatbush Avenue. He usually disappeared after work on Sundays, and I wouldn't see him until Tuesday. Sometimes I covered for him so he could split early, then later punched his timecard with mine.

It was another of my idle Mondays. I'd just stepped away from a curbside coffee stand with a steaming cup and a bagel. On the opposite side of the street a jackhammer crew was destroying the macadam, preparing the ground for a new sewer line. There must have been a half-dozen burly guys in hardhats pounding furiously. Between their noise and the subway roaring overhead the decibel level was like the firing range at Dix.

A Surf Avenue bus stopped on their side of the street and several people stepped down, including a young blonde woman. She quickly came within range, walking into the construction zone where stanchions had marked off a narrow path through the chaos. She was absolutely the most beautiful woman I'd ever seen. She wore spike heels that shifted her hips with every step. She carried herself erect, almost queenly, striding confidently on killer legs. The machine-gun rattle of the jackhammers went silent, replaced by whistles and catcalls: "It's Doctor Susie!" "Hey, Doctor Susie, please marry me, I can be divorced in two weeks!" "I love youse, Doctor Susie!" "Doctor Susie, please sit on my face!"

She strode on, eyes straight ahead, pirouetting adroitly to avoid the sweaty hands reaching for her ass, stoic expression never changing. On coming even with the entrance of the marine laboratory she climbed the few steps to the door and disappeared inside. A collective groan arose from the street as blood once again flowed through constricted arteries, and frantic hearts recovered from minor cardiac arrest.

Reluctantly, the jackhammers coughed to life, except one. Its operator lit a cigarette and leaned on the handle. I walked over. "Who was that?"

He turned and looked at me. "Doctor Susie. She's a marine biologist at the lab and studies fish or something. What a waste, huh? Man, some fox." He shook his head.

That evening I mentioned to Angel about having seen her. "Ah, Doctor Susie." Angel put the fingers of one hand together and kissed the tips. "Every straight guy that's still got lead in his pencil has wet dreams about her. She's the fox of all foxes."

"That's what the guys with jackhammers say. They're all barking about jumping her."

"Them sweathogs destroying Surf Avenue? Not even in their most outrageous fantasies. They might have better luck wit a skank like Liz Taylor. Doctor Susie seems untouchable."

The director of the lab was a doctor too, but also a Jesuit priest, born and raised in Brooklyn. His parents had immigrated from Sicily. His given name was Giuseppe, or Joseph in English, and everyone in the neighborhood knew him as Father Joe. He was a happy hour regular at Catalano's where everything for him was on the house, including dinner with all the amenities. He was an upbeat, friendly guy, always smiling and slapping backs and bantering with the staff in Italian. People were eager to shake his hand, as if it might get them closer to the Almighty. If you were a stranger and walked in off the street you might easily think he was a local politician or maybe owned the place because he was dressed in a business suit, not the standard priestly garb.

I noticed him right away. It was hard not to. The guy had undeniable presence. Then Angel told me how it is with Catholics. The free goodies represent an unofficial "indulgence," a sort of religious bribe that the owners, by making this round-about donation to the church through the earthly personage of Father Joe, believed they were lessening the time of their future torment in purgatory. The owners, he said, thought of their largess as a sort of get-out-of-jail-early card, operationally similar to an E-ZPass on the Jersey Turnpike where you pay the fees up front and zip right past the toll takers. "Trust me," he said, "these bozos need all the help they can get. Their chance at heaven is the same as going to the track and betting on a three-legged horse to place.

"Anyhow, they're stupid and don't got a clue about indulgences, which in real life can only be approved by a bishop. Sucking up to a parish priest—which the good Father ain't even—don't get youse points along the highway to Salvation. I know 'cause I got a cousin who's a priest and I ast him about it."

But Father Joe provided another benefit to Catalano's, if only occasionally. If one of the regulars had sinned and felt exceptionally guilty a waiter would whisper news of his anguish to Father Joe. He'd slide off his barstool, take a priest's tab collar from his suitcoat pocket, and disappear into the kitchen where two chairs had already been dragged in from the dining area. The sudden appearance of Father Joe and another guy was a signal for everyone in the kitchen to split for the alley or storeroom because Father Joe was about to hear an impromptu confession. Waiters and bussers trapped in the dining area stayed there, and Giovanni went around to customers awaiting their dinners, apologizing and telling everyone there was a small problem with the gas in the kitchen, and their meals would be delayed. However, the bar was open if anyone required a refill.

Nearly all these penitents were wiseguys, Mafia foot soldiers. Naturally, the kitchen staff could only guess as to their sudden need of absolution. Maybe, as Angel speculated, they were afraid of getting whacked before they could confess in an actual church, although on one occasion we learned the reason.

It was a slow night in January. On the appearance of

Father Joe and a wiseguy we recognized as a regular at the bar we had grabbed our coats and stepped outside into falling snow. Meanwhile, the chefs had shut down the grill, ovens, and stoves and along with the sous chefs and bussers were squeezing into the storeroom.

A frigid breeze crawled through the alley and crept underneath our clothes. The sodium streetlamps cast the world in cruel sepia and painted our faces the gray-green pallor of death. Mario and Margarito, the two Guatemalan guys, grabbed wine crates and took shelter on the downwind side of the dumpster while Angel and I huddled outside the kitchen door and lit up. Because of the weather Surf Avenue and its sidewalks were nearly vacant. The night was quiet except when a train rattled past overhead. It was near midnight.

The wiseguy giving confession was Willie White Eyes, known by that name because parts of the irises of his eyes had been depigmented since birth, leaving sections of them white. The mosaic of brown interspersed with white gave his eyes an odd appearance but apparently didn't affect his vision. Still, he wore sunglasses most of the time, indoors or out. Willie's other notable characteristic was his unusually loud voice. The man didn't know the definition of whisper, and even during a busy happy hour his voice in normal conversation floated above everyone else's. From where Angel and I stood Father Joe's words were muted by the metal door, but Willie's could not have been clearer.

His confession had to do with the recent murder of a Mafia goon in Queens, a wiseguy well known to the authorities. The event had been in the news for several days. One smart-aleck radio commentator had added his own exaggerated spin, reporting that the body recovered from the East River had been wrapped in heavy chain and that taped inside the mouth was a canary, a message from the mob of what happens to squealers. The commentator paused before concluding in a deadpan voice, "The cops suspect foul play."

Angel whispered the probable scene in the kitchen: Willie on his knees before Father Joe or maybe sitting in the other chair facing him. As Angel explained later, to initiate a confession Willie first must have made the sign of the cross. Then we heard him say, "Forgive me Father, for I have sinned. I can't remember my last confession. It's been a long time." Father Joe then mumbled something inaudible, and we listened in fascination—along with everyone in the restaurant who wasn't deaf—in Willie's voice how he and Lenny the Lurch, another regular patron, had carried out a hit on a mob guy from a different Mafia family in Queens. How they crept up on him one night, shot him behind the ear, stuffed the body in the trunk of their car, and then tossed it in the river. How the guy, in Willie's words, "was a squealing scumbag motherfucker and deserved it." Father Joe reminded him that he and Lenny had violated the Fifth Commandment, and to kill another human is a mortal sin. Willie choked up and blurted, "I'm so goddamn sorry, Father!" Angel looked at me. He rolled his eyes and made a motion like he was jacking off. "Perfect," he whispered sarcastically.

Father Joe evidently assigned penance of three Hail Marys because Willie practically shouted them to everyone in Brooklyn still awake, and to pray an Act of Contrition, which Willie couldn't remember, so Father Joe recited a suitable prayer line for line while Willie tried his best between sobs to repeat it. Father Joe then said the Prayer of Absolution, some of which we could make out. Willie said, "Amen," and the chairs scraped back. A minute later Giovanni peeked out the door, and we went inside.

The rest of the night was a dud. Catalano's stayed open, but only a few customers came. We cleaned up the kitchen and punched out around one. Renato was straightening up his bar area. He said, "Hey, you boys wanna sumting to warma the blood? Itsa cold out tonight." We slid onto stools, and he poured each of us a shot of Jack Daniel's and one for himself. Those were so satisfying he poured another round.

Outside, we started walking. The wind had picked up, and snowflakes mingled with trash swirled around us. Angel shivered. "I gotta get some different shoes and socks. My feet are fucking freezing." Then abruptly he changed the subject. "Know what I don't get? Some stuff in Willie's confession ain't logical. I think he was bullshitting Papa J. Take the kill shot. To plug somebody behind the ear youse gotta be close, like inches. Real life ain't like a cowboy movie where the guy in the white hat is so deadly he shoots the gun outta the bad guy's hand. Ha! Willie and Lenny? Gimme a break.

"So, either they was buddied up wit the victim, walking along wit him, say, or they snuck up on him from behind. Buddies is unlikely. There's been bad blood between the two families since I was a kid. As to the second possibility, them two knuckle-heads couldn't sneak up on a corpse, not wit Lenny the Lurch on the team. You seen how he drags that club foot along, banging it into everything like it's stuck in a mop bucket. He sometimes waves his arms like a spaz to keep his balance. Waiters and bussers carrying loaded trays know to jump back five feet so's not to get caught in his stumble-bum windmill. When in motion he takes up the space of a crowd, for chrissakes, and sounds like the brass section in his own personal parade. Sneak up on another wiseguy? Only if he's deaf.

"Then to hoist the dead guy into the trunk of a car, drive to the docks, haul him out, roll him in fifty pounds of chain, and heave him in the river? Him and Willie? C'mon, no way. That takes muscle. Maybe if the target is a midget, which I seriously doubt. The *capos* don't put little monkeys on the payroll. They prefer big gorillas wit brains the size of walnuts. Sometimes wiseguy work requires heavy lifting, and in that department Willie and Lenny is wimps, and Lenny being a crip don't help in this regard. Them two together, they don't match up to youse average civilian sofa spud, musclewise. Naw, there's gotta more to the story than what Willie tells Father Joe."

But if there really was anything else, we never found out about it.

Chapter 2

—••—

I WAS STANDING IN line at Nathan's Famous on the boardwalk on a sunny Monday morning in spring looking forward to a chili dog and a cold beer when something wrapped itself around my leg. I looked down suspecting entanglement in a dog leash, but it wasn't that, it was a little girl. She was two or three, somewhere in that range. She said, "Daddy!" and gazed up at me with blue eyes that were too big for her face. A young woman, evidently the mother, was squatting down trying to pry the child's arms from my leg, but she had a grip like an octopus. I saw just the mother's back and a head thatched with thick brown hair. After unwrapping the kid she stood and pushed her hair away from her face. "I'm sorry," she said, and I looked into her daughter's future adult eyes, perfectly in proportion. "I'm sorry," she repeated. "This is so embarrassing."

I made a joke, saying now that we were acquainted we might as well introduce ourselves. She told me her name was Julie, that this "assailant," as she put it, was her daughter Amy, who was three. I asked if I could buy them lunch, and she shyly accepted, telling me I was very generous considering I'd just been the victim of a random attack on the boardwalk right in front of witnesses. Afterward, we walked a while, and when Amy got tired and started rubbing her eyes I picked her up, and she fell asleep on my shoulder. Passersby probably thought we were a happy little family out for a stroll beside the beach.

Conversation with Julie was easy. Her parents were dead, and she had no living relatives except Amy. She and her husband had moved to Brooklyn from Pennsylvania, and then about six months later he and a woman in the office where he worked had taken off together, to where Julie had no idea. She was on her own, just starting a job as cashier in a bank. She and Amy had been forced to move to a cheaper apartment, now having to make ends meet on a single salary. A retired woman down the hall babysat Amy during weekdays. Julie and I had met by chance only because that particular Monday was a bank holiday. Any other Monday and she'd have been at work. I said maybe we were lucky. She looked down and smiled, then reached up and stroked Amy's hair.

I walked them home, still carrying the baby. They lived in a second-floor unit in a building a street over from where Angel and I lived. The walls were dull and needing paint, the carpet threadbare. The living room was furnished with a crib, tattered couch, and two stained armchairs. There was a phone on the wall. She gave me the number. I told her I lived with a roomie in a hotel nearby, and we didn't have a phone. Anyway, there was no point calling, I said, because the desk clerks seldom answered, and if they did they declined to leave messages for us "guests." I said the last word with a laugh.

I'd mentioned to her earlier that I worked at Catalano's. She said she knew it but never had been inside. I told her I was a dishwasher. I try to be truthful so people don't expect too much from me. I am what you see: average-looking, poor, and mostly honest without too many bad habits and a history that doesn't require being locked away out of sight. If anything, my life has been boring.

Julie was quite attractive and, as I was discovering, intelligent, pleasant, and even-tempered, never complaining about the shit sandwich life had handed her. I told her I worked afternoons and nights with Mondays off, sometimes not leaving Catalano's until one or two in the morning. We made a date for the coming Friday after the restaurant closed. She said she couldn't go out, there was no one to watch Amy at night, but I was welcome to stop by. I said I'd bring two Italian dinners if she didn't mind staying up late.

I told Angel about Julie and Amy and asked if I could split early on Friday. I needed two dinners to go with the works. He said sure, that I'd been covering for him on Sundays so he could bop off to spend nights with Maria. I called Julie and said to have the oven hot for reheating by eleven-thirty, that I was leaving around eleven. When I ducked out I was toting a Catalano's take-away bag containing veal parmesan and chicken piccata entrées, a container of grated parmesan, salads with vinaigrette dressing on the side, a dinner-sized loaf of freshly baked bread, two servings of tiramisú, and a nearly full bottle of chianti, all of it gratis. I didn't realize until unpacking everything that Angel and the chefs had included a candle.

We were hitting it off pretty well. The three of us were together nearly every Monday starting in the afternoon after Julie got home from work and went down the hall to get Amy. I'd spend the night at her place, and occasionally other nights too, depending on how busy the restaurant was and how my social calendar meshed with Angel's. He was still seeing Maria, although not talking much about it.

Summer was over, replaced by beautiful fall weather. The local scene had become less crowded, although the eternal sordidness synonymous with Coney Island continued unchanged. In the perpetual twilight among the forest of pilings holding up the boardwalk was a hidden city: men who lurked near the stairs naked except for raincoats, fixated on flashing the women walking to and from the beach; hookers hustling a quick lay, and men, women, and those of uncertain gender offering blowjobs; pimps, panhandlers, winos, junkies, drug dealers, thieves, the insane, the homeless; harmless pickpockets and vicious thugs looking to roll somebody. All of them random souls who for multiple reasons had found themselves trapped in this peculiar gravitational field. And all the while oblivious tourists strolled overhead laughing and licking ice-cream cones.

I was doing favors for Julie, which I could tell she truly appreciated. One Monday morning on another bank holiday we went to a paint store where she picked out some colors she liked. I bought a few gallons in latex and repainted her apartment: white ceilings all around, beige walls for the living room, a bright yellow for the kitchen, and lime green for the bathroom. On another day before work I went alone to a hardware store and later replaced her electrical outlets, grounding them all, and installed new light switches. She was thrilled, moreso knowing the building's superintendent would never do it. I even fixed her babysitter's toilet, which ran continuously and kept her awake. She expressed shock and gratitude when I refused payment and told Julie then and there that I was a keeper.

This all boosted my ego, which throughout my life had languished in a dark place. Still, underneath the thin veneer of happiness was the same chronic doubt and the queasy feeling that I was getting too close to Julie and Amy, that unpleasantness loomed. It was fear of commitment submerged underneath the ugly reality of knowing myself, realizing I would never amount to anything. I had no ambition, no interest in rising in the world; ergo, I was unworthy of having a family and hefting responsibility for anyone else. In feeling like this I was cruising on a level plane at the same altitude as Angel.

He and I were on a smoke break in the alley one night. I asked how it was going with Maria and her son, who was around eight. "It's going," he said, "but where? Who knows. She's busting my balls to move wit her back to Puerto Rico, some little village in the mountains where nobody wears shoes and the whole population probably has hookworms. A place where youse open the taps on the sink and only air comes out; the toilets don't flush, mosquitoes is everywhere, dirt streets turn to mud in the rain. Fuck that, I say to her. Then she gets pissed and nags me, telling me I'm just a dishwasher wit no ambition, and I'm selfish 'cause I don't consider her needs. Both things is true, but that ain't the whole picture, okay? Then I ast her about jobs in this hick town of Santa Marta. I remind her that according to her own descriptions of it there ain't a restaurant having dishes to wash even if I wanted to, just food stands crawling wit flies and roaches and youse can die of the ptomaine. So what would I do for money? In fact, I say, there ain't a goddamn thing in this Santa Marta except youse parents and some other toothless relatives youse is homesick for, God knows why." He looked at me and grinned. "It must be sorta like West Virginia, although I ain't been to either place."

I said, "It seems familiar."

"Then there's something else, the big gray elephant in the room." He dropped his cigarette butt and stepped on it.

"Which is?"

"The same elephant that's looking at youse if youse keep hanging out wit this broad Julie and her kid. It's simple, just hard to accept. I ain't prepared to take on a family, and from what I seen in our time together, neither is youse."

"Why not? You might like having a family. Maybe you'd be good at it."

"No, I'd be terrible. I'd fail for sure. Plus, Maria and me obviously don't get along that good, and the kid puts pressure on me to be, youse know, a daddy." He looked at me directly. "I don't know much, but I know this: down deep I'm irresponsible when it comes to relationships and always will be. Sure, I can fake it for a time, but in the end something cracks. The woman's expectations and mine get out of whack, and I split. At that point I don't want no baggage dragging behind me. I like it loose and alone. Basically, I'm satisfied wit my life, and the minute I try to, as they say, 'better myself' that's the minute I ain't myself no more, meaning I ain't satisfied no more neither."

I flipped my cigarette butt into the alley, and we went inside. It was a lot to think about. However, I was feeling optimistic. Julie and I never argued or even exchanged harsh words. She was sweet, kind, and honest, and Amy was a treat.

Julie was earning pretty good money at the bank, and suddenly her husband was in our conversations, how she intended to track him down and start divorce proceedings. She wanted to break free. I knew that if we became a family—and we surely were sliding toward that—I'd need to "better myself" for sake of our collective security. There could be no avoiding it. Dishwashing as a career is possible only if you stay single and push back any dreams of upward mobility. Clearly, that was Angel, but was it me? Knowing myself as I did, could the sacrifice necessary to gain a family be justified considering the high probability of failure? And it wouldn't involve just my sacrifice, but Julie's and Amy's too.

Amy was disarming, and I felt a vague unease around her. She seemed able to penetrate the phony self I projected and dive directly into the dark crevices of my soul. Once inside she probed around and found me untrustworthy, peripatetic, and grotesquely self-ish. She discovered a caricature offering emptiness instead of empathy, sadness instead of surety. Or so I imagined, and that it made me nervous meant I saw myself this way. I couldn't be certain about what Amy actually thought. Maybe I was being overly paranoid, attributing too much to what likely were guileless mannerisms, but for a three-year-old Amy came across as preternaturally perceptive and wise.

Summer had come around again. I'd been seeing Julie and Amy for a little more than a year. Amy carried a stuffed toy with her everywhere. It was a rabbit, as I recall, and on this particular day she resembled a little stuffed animal herself in her pink sleeping suit with feet, and bows on the sides of her head that made the bundled hair stand up like ears.

She and I were sitting together on the couch when I asked her the rabbit's name. She said it was a secret. I told her she could trust me, but she turned away. "I can't trust anybody," she said quietly.

"Does Mommy or Daddy know its name?"

"No. Just me." She seemed thoughtful, as if pondering a decision, then stood and said, "I had a daddy, but he runned away. He told me he wouldn't do that." Fat tears rolled out of her enormous blue eyes, magnifying them still more. She sniffled then leaned closer and whispered, "I'll tell you its name if you promise to stay."

Something gave in my chest. I suddenly felt weak and useless as if all my life I'd been taking up space like any loser. Really, what was I doing with my life? Where was it going? I sensed a vague kinship with Amy's deadbeat father. Leaving his wife and little daughter was a rotten act. I rationalized it by trying to convince myself that I didn't know their story, so who was I to judge? Julie, to her credit, never complained about him or cut him down. Perhaps those pure of heart gain sainthood by suffering stoically through the worst of times and not becoming demeaned by their circumstances. Maybe this guy was a decent person, although deep inside I knew better. My vision blurred, and I realized I was crying too, big silent sobs of pity for Amy and her mother, for him, for me, for the whole goddamn world. I kissed Amy's forehead, then left without waiting to say anything to Julie, who was in the bathroom. I simply left. I never phoned or went back.

Chapter 3

———••———

WHAT I'D JUST DONE—ABRUPTLY dumping Julie and Amy—was freaking me out. I couldn't sleep. I was chain-smoking and drinking too much. For three nights running following work I sat in the room sipping bourbon straight from the bottle until eventually toppling over shitfaced. Angel was at Maria's those times, but he'd see me the next day and knew I was hurting. When he asked what was bothering me I told him. I said the guilt was dragging me under, that I thought I was drowning. I was ashamed, I said. I had run away from a terrific woman and a little girl and in doing this behaved like, well, a little girl. I wasn't man enough to admit that Amy was likely more mature than I ever would be.

"Youse ain't seen or talked to them since just walking out? Well, so what? Why the heavy guilt? Youse sound like a Catholic. People break up all the time. Get over it. Youse done the right thing, considering the alternative, 'cause let's face it, youse ain't husband

and daddy material. That's the truth of things. It's what we are, me and youse."

He was right, of course, but it didn't relieve that shitty feeling deep down each time I pictured Amy on the couch crying, and probably Julie crying too after I'd left. What I needed was a change of scenery. My second autumn in Coney Island had come around again, and it seemed an appropriate time to move on. A new place, a new life. I know the old saying that you can't leave yourself behind, that your conscience sticks to you like a shadow, but I dreaded bumping into Julie and Amy on the street by chance. What would I say, that I'm sorry I'm a weasel, that y'all are better off with me out of your lives? That I would have failed you eventually anyway? I found myself looking over my shoulder, prepared to duck into a side street or pull up my coat collar and walk low, crawl even, trying to make myself small; better yet, invisible. It's stupid, I know, but I felt like a hunted man.

I moped around for a week feeling crappy and disgusted with myself. Then Angel said, "I got just what youse need, a date wit my kid sister. She's a live wire, always upbeat. She'll give youse a attitude adjustment. Youse and her might hit it off and end up getting married. And then youse would be my brother-in-law. What could be better?"

"I'll probably think of something."

He clapped me on the back. "Aw, don't be so negative. Angelina's a smart, good-looking *chica*. Youse is gonna be impressed, guaranteed."

Generally, it isn't a good idea to go along when a guy offers to fix you up with his sister. You're always thinking, what's the catch? Girls who are vivacious and pretty are usually popular. If so, why would she agree to a blind date? I was skeptical but went anyway.

Angelina lived with their parents in the Brooklyn neighborhood of Bedford-Stuyvesant, or Bed-Stuy, in New York slang. Angel warned me to be careful, the area could be dangerous. Don't loiter or look around too much. He advised going directly to the apartment building, which was a block from the subway stop. The family lived on the third floor, number 327. Enter the first set of doors then ring the bell to get buzzed into the foyer. They would be expecting me. It was a Monday evening, our day off from the restaurant.

Angelina was home alone, her parents out at a movie. She was nineteen going on thirteen with big brown eyes and a ponytail, all giggles and squeals and yelps and sentences ending in question marks. We hopped in a taxi, and she took me to a local club where the clientele was a hundred percent Puerto Rican. She knew everyone. No standing in line for us. She grabbed my hand, blew a kiss to the hulk guarding the entrance, and we slithered like eels through the waiting crowd into an arena that could have doubled as an airplane hangar. It was so big that it held two bands, one at each end, both blasting Latin music. The thick smoky air scavenged sounds like a sponge sucking up spilled beer, damping reverberations but holding captive every note and murmur. Conversation required shouting directly into the other person's ear, then leaning in with your ear to receive the response.

There were several free-standing bars scattered around. Customers waiting for drinks at the one closest to us stood three deep. They were all guys. Angelina crooked a finger at me, a signal, I supposed, to lean down. Her lips were warm against my ear. "I know the bartender. What are youse drinking?" I touched my lips to her ear. "A beer," I said, and handed her a five. She elbowed to the very front, smiling and acknowledging those she displaced with a laugh and lips-to-ear comments. They didn't appear to mind her rude intrusion, smiling back and sometimes giving her a peck on the cheek.

As I stood there vaguely taking in the scene a memory returned. Actually, it was more a feeling, a state of mind, the one time I'd lost control and toppled for an instant over the edge into insanity. It happened in seventh grade. There was a big kid in class named Erwin. He had been flunked twice, ought to have been in high school, and was outsized even for his own age group. Erwin was a mouth-breather, and his mouth was always open because of adenoid problems or something. When he breathed he made soft gurgling noises.

Erwin also was a bully, and I and the other boys were nervous around him. He was followed everywhere by a cadre of sycophants who snickered on cue when he alerted them to something funny or demeaning he'd just said.

I stammered badly as a kid. Stammering and stuttering are different. A stutterer repeats a sound in staccato fashion; a stammerer has difficulty getting the sound out, which leads to making odd facial expressions during the effort, often spewing distracting and incomprehensible noises, substituting difficult words

with misapplied synonyms that are easier to enunci-
ate, and even foot-stamping in an effort to expel the
desired word, usually one starting with a consonant.

Language is supposed to be fluid and spontaneous,
not an exercise in agony. The inability to speak dam-
ages your confidence and ultimately singes your soul.
The spoken word becomes a minefield where every
utterance is accompanied by possible ridicule and
rejection. My stammer dissipated after I joined the
Army. I simply outgrew it, I guess. However, some
of the collateral damage remains residual and never
goes away.

Anyway, several of us were standing around on
the school grounds one morning waiting for the bell
to ring when I tried to say something. This was an
unusual occurrence because ordinarily I was reticent to
speak at all and lived encased inside a woeful silence
that made me seem even more timid. In this instance
I couldn't get the intended word past my lips and
contorted my face in the attempt. Erwin shoved me
to the ground and started to laugh, which cued his
bunch of ass kissers to laugh too. The bell rang, and
he turned toward the door. For reasons I still don't
understand I ran at him and buried my head in his
midsection, which was a bit flabby. He gasped and
fell to the ground, the wind knocked out of him. I
jumped on his stomach and started pummeling his
face with my fists. Blood squirted out his nose, but
I kept pounding him relentlessly. He could easily
have pushed me off, but instead lay there passively
weeping and begging me to stop. Finally, a couple
of teachers, wondering why some of us hadn't come

inside, showed up and pulled me away. My rage, however, was boundless, and I tried to take them on too, swinging wildly at them, at the air, at anything until they finally pinned my arms to my sides. I was insane with rage, not screaming or yelling but focused intently on beating Erwin to mush. It must have been a synesthetic event because my mental state was manifested as a kaleidoscope of colors.

That happened only once, but I now felt a strange tremor as if the sensation was about to be reprised. I couldn't let it happen. Angelina returned with the drinks accompanied by four guys, evidently members of her crowd because they were talking and laughing, everyone but me high on good fellowship. She handed me the beer and the change, and we coalesced into a tight circle the better to hear each other, not that I had anything to offer.

One of the guys leaned close to my ear. Angelina, he said, had told the group that I was from West Virginia. I nodded. He said he hadn't known that West Virginia was even a place, then stepped back and laughed as if he'd said something funny. I put my hand on his shoulder. He offered his ear, and I said, "You mean, sort of like Puerto Rico?" I felt my heartbeat quicken, my blood pressure rise.

He stepped back and shot me an unpleasant look. I returned it with an evil grin and a shrug, emphasizing I couldn't give a rat-fuck what he thought. He whispered something to Angelina, who looked at me with something like disgust. I told her I thought we should leave, that this place was annoying. She shook her head and suggested I go and she would catch a ride home with her friends. That was fine with me. She gave one of those cutesy waves holding her hand waist-high, palm out, and oscillating back and forth like a windshield wiper. Then she turned and literally ran into the crowd. She didn't look back.

I went outside and asked the hulk guarding the door directions to the closest subway stop. He told me in halting English that I wasn't safe walking to it alone. He yelled something in Spanish to a group of guys standing around smoking. One of them broke away and sauntered over. The two had a conversation in rapid Spanish. The guy turned to me and said in English, "Jorge ast us to walk youse to the subway. We're headed there too. He's right that it ain't safe for gringos. This here's our neighborhood and won't nobody fuck witchuse wit us around."

———————

I told Angel I was quitting the restaurant and hitting the open road. He asked if I had a plan. No plan, I said. He asked what I would do once I arrived at this unknown place, wherever it was. I said I didn't know that either, but wherever it was the weather would be warm, and I wouldn't be leaving work every day with dishpan hands. Maybe get back into auto mechanics, something like that.

When I told Giuseppe he did something entirely unexpected: he hugged me and cried. "I don't wanta you to go! You always treated me witha respect. I'ma gonna miss you. Come back anytime, always a job here. If I had a son I wanta him to be like you."

Word spread to the bar crowd, and several of the

wiseguys said they were sorry to see me go, but bet I'd be back. There's no better place than Coney Island. This was paradise. They bought me drinks and said to hang loose. When I told them I'd be heading south with my thumb out, Willie White Eyes spoke up.

"Can youse be ready to travel by tomorrow?"

"Sure," I said.

"I'm visiting my mom in Jersey, and I could give youse the first lift, at least get youse away from the city. She lives in New Brunswick. There's a big truck stop on Route 1 where youse is sure to get a ride. Be in front of the restaurant at ten sharp."

Willie was driving a shiny '58 Chevy Impala two-door, turquois with a white hardtop, whitewalls, and turquois fender skirts. I tossed my backpack onto the rear seat and jumped into the passenger side. "Beautiful car," I said.

Willie said, "Thanks. That's it?" He jerked his thumb over his shoulder at my luggage. "Youse is moving to a whole other state wit just a backpack? Jesus, wish I could do that. If I ever leave Coney Island it'll be wit a fleet of vans hauling all my shit. Unbelievable, the junk I've piled up, and I ain't even married wit kids." He shook his head. "I take it youse ain't in a rush, seeing how youse don't even know the, uh, the destination."

I nodded. "Good, 'cause I gotta deliver a package in Jersey City. That's north before we go south to New Brunswick." I said it was fine with me. I didn't ask what was in the package. It might have been anything from a batch of homemade cookies to a severed head. Along the way we discussed the two subjects dearest to men's hearts, sex and money, and how hardly anybody ever gets enough of either. Actually, Willie did the majority of talking. I've always been better at listening.

"I do pretty good wit the ladies," he said, "but take Lenny the Lurch, my compadre. He's sort of a sad sack, dragging around that club foot. Makes it tough for him to chase down pussy. Once in a while he manages to pick off a straggler, one that don't run so good." He looked sideways to see if I got the joke, and when I smiled he guffawed and pounded the steering wheel. "Just wondering if youse would catch on, being a hillbilly. Them mountain chicks, is it true they're generally knocked up by fourteen?"

"Thirteen, and we keep them barefoot."

Willie laughed. "Know how people always say that things come out even in the long run, a guy takes strike three in one aspect of life and hits it out of the park in another? That's Lenny. The poor bastid hardly ever gets laid, but know what? He might have the biggest schlong in Brooklyn, maybe all of New York. Ever notice that guys standing at a row of urinals is always sneaking glances at the peckers of the guys next to them? It's 'cause everybody is curious how he measures up.

"Well, one day me and Lenny is on a stakeout, car backed into this alley so's we can scan the street. Our bladders is the size of basketballs from all the coffee. Lenny says, 'I gotta water my horse,' and I says, 'likewise.' We step outta the car to take a piss against the building, and when Lenny finishes hauling out his schvantz I swear it hangs down nearly a foot. I ain't shitting youse." He shook his head in wonder. "And I'm thinking, hell, wit that equipment I could rule the world, or at least the Italian section of Coney Island. The Jewish section, probably not 'cause Lenny ain't circumcised. He's a genuine fur-bearing animal, motoring through life wit one head still wearing its birth hat, the other wit a full mop of hair, lucky guy. Me, I'm bald as a cueball, both my heads. Lenny, it's the head between his legs that's the possible celebrity. The other one is used mostly as a hat rack.

"Reminds me of a joke. Two guys get off a plane at La Guardia and make a beeline for the men's room. They're standing side by side, and one guy says, 'Hey, I notice youse is tattooed wit WE. I bet it says WENDY 'cause that's what I got tattooed on mine. Wendy's my girlfriend.' The other guy, he says, 'Naw, I work for the Chamber of Commerce. Youse is seeing just the tip. When I pull all of it out and it stands up and gets angry, the whole message says, WELCOME TO NEW YORK HOPE YOUSE HAS A WONDERFUL DAY IN THE CITY. Ain't that a scream? I told that joke a hunnert times, and it still cracks me up." He pounded the steering wheel again and laughed until tiny little tears squeezed out from underneath the sunglasses.

He turned toward me. "I hardly hear a word outta youse. Not a talker, huh?"

"I'd rather listen. Everybody has more to say than me. You, for example. These are great stories."

"I bet youse didn't know I'm a businessman. Being a wiseguy is my day job—well, sometimes nights too, depending on the assignment and workload. My two brothers and me, we're in the parking lot profession. Ever notice that parking lot on West 16th Street? The guy running it is my brother Larry. He sits in that little booth collecting money. My other brother Frankie, he's the accountant and keeps the books. He went to college to learn how. People pay a premium to park so close to the boardwalk and beach, a five-minute walk. Youse ain't said nuttin. Never noticed our lot?"

"No."

"Really?

"Maybe if I was a car owner."

"Right. Anyhow, youse might of wondered how much a booming operation like ours pays the mob for protection. I'll tell youse. Not a dime. Why? 'Cause I *am* the mob. It's sort of a corporate benefit. Naturally, being a part owner I park this baby for free, and Larry sees that its kept covered wit a custom tarp." He tapped the steering wheel lovingly.

"When I ain't busy I sometimes take over for Larry to give him a break. He keeps a .38 underneath the cash drawer, but not being a violent sort he ain't never used it. Instead, he has a baseball bat leaning in the corner, just in case. A honest businessman can't be too careful in Coney Island wit low-lifes everywheres— thieves, junkies, loonies, drug dealers. The cops at the 60th know about Larry. He cracks heads wit the best and don't take nobody's shit. That bat handle is mostly notches. The cops, they'd rather business owners solve their own problems, right? Less paperwork for them, right? The cops, they tell Larry, just try not to kill nobody. Broken skulls is sometimes the cost of doing business, and we get that, but somebody dies?

The fucking paperwork will bury us."

He lit a cigar and exhaled smoke through his nostrils. He glanced at the cigar, then over at me. "I oughta quit these. People say they're unhealthy."

"It's a myth."

"What?"

"It's probably bullshit." I lit a cigarette.

"Right. Commie propaganda to make Americans look like losers."

"No doubt."

He settled back on the seat. "The barflies at Catalano's couldn't understand youse at first wit that hillbilly accent, but we got usta it. Turned out youse ain't the retard we thought. College?"

"A year at junior college."

"Hell, youse got more education than the whole bar lineup at Catalano's, 'cepting Father Joe, of course. He's a doctor of some kind and also went to priest college. Then youse quit?"

"A year was enough. It taught me how to read— what I mean is, how to tell good writing from trash and how to appreciate literature. Once you learn that you're able to teach yourself as you go through life, adding to your education book by book. I still have a lot to learn. Then two years in the Army, mostly at Dix, where they trained me to be a mechanic. I was hoping to get transferred overseas so I could see some of the world, but no luck."

"Damn, so youse ended up a dishwasher. Weird." I told him about Robbie, Angel's cousin, and the phantom job at a garage that never materialized because the place was a front for a chop-shop, that Robbie's uncle who owned it went to jail.

We arrived in Jersey City and pulled up at a restaurant that could have been Catalano's twin. Willie gave me a five and said to get two coffees, his light with double sugars, and bagels with cream cheese at a diner across the street, then wait in the car. He took a box from the trunk and went into the restaurant. It didn't seem particularly heavy, maybe twenty pounds tops. I'd read somewhere that an average adult human head weighs around fourteen pounds. There could have been a severed head inside, or else a helluva lot of homemade cookies. He was gone about ten minutes. After he returned I gave him the change, and we sat there another fifteen minutes or so sipping coffee and munching bagels. He said, "I don't know where youse will end up, but youse will never find bagels so good as in New York and Jersey."

He set me out at the New Brunswick truck stop, then leaned over and rolled down the window on the passenger side. We shook hands and said our good-byes and good lucks, and I was turning to walk away when I heard, "Hey, c'mere." He leaned toward the window and handed me a fifty dollar bill. I said it wasn't necessary, but he waved me away like it was peanuts.

"Thanks, that's really generous," I said. "I forgot to mention that I hear an engine noise I don't like. Keep an eye on the temperature gauge and get your water pump replaced. It's about to go. And make sure the antifreeze stays at full strength year-around. Anyone at a gas station can check that for you."

"Holy hell. Thanks!" And he was off. It was mid-afternoon.

I went into the diner and had the trucker's blue-plate special, then used the restroom. I needed some smaller bills and paid with the fifty. Afterward, I stood at the exit and stuck out my thumb. Right away a big rig stopped and waved me aboard. "South or north?" the driver said, and I said south. He nodded and revved up. "Me too."

Thumbing from a truck stop is almost always a better way of hitching rides than standing roadside. This driver was gracious and dropped me at a truck stop outside Richmond even though he didn't need diesel and had planned to blow right past it.

My luck flagged somewhat after that. Thumbing is always unpredictable. The next driver let me out at a nowhere intersection south of Raleigh just as it started to rain. I stood shivering, wet as a muskrat for three or four hours before a traveling salesman took pity and pulled over. He rolled down the window on the passenger side and said he was going as far as Rocking- ham. I told him I was soaked and didn't want to mess up his car, but he said not to worry, it was a company car and if he didn't score some sales in Rockingham he'd be out of a job and a car too. He was a nice guy and told me his life story as we cruised through what morphed into a monsoon. By the time we reached Rockingham the rain was done, I was somewhat dry, and we were sharing a bottle of bourbon.

At my request the salesman dropped me at a truck stop where I changed clothes and got a hot meal. I stood at the exit for a couple of hours before a trucker signaled me aboard. He was headed to Savannah and eventually would leave Route 1 at Augusta on the state line with South Carolina, explaining that Route 1 veers southwest from there down to Wadley, then southeast to Waycross. I was welcome to ride to Savannah if I didn't mind some stop-and-go on county roads. I looked at my map. From Savannah it probably made sense to continue on back roads south to Jacksonville and pick up Route 1 again there. Having heard that Savannah was an interesting place, I said okay, I didn't have anything better to do.

Chapter 4

———••———

THE SAVANNAH TRUCK STOP was huge, one of those places where truckers can shower and shave, do their laundry, even rent a cheap room and sack out for a few hours, a welcome break from sleeping in their cabs. I was beat and took full advantage of all these amenities. Rested and clean, I went to the diner and ordered the "trucker's breakfast" of three eggs accompanied by three pancakes plus sausage, bacon, grits, toast, and coffee. I added a slice of apple pie. The waitress told me that Savanah has lots of small parks, and if I wanted to see some of those and the famous Southern mansions that a bus came through regularly. I hopped aboard and asked the driver to pick a good spot near a park to let me off, that I wanted to see some of the big houses and those live oaks with Spanish moss.

It was about nine in the morning. The sun was out, and the day was warming up. I walked around looking at everything and noticed a pile of cordwood in one of the yards. A few extra dollars never hurt. I knocked on the door, and a large Black woman opened it. She was wearing a house dress, slippers, and a bandanna over her head. She looked me up and down and said, "Whatchu want? We ain't feeding no bums here."

I took off my baseball cap and gave a slight bow. "Sorry to bother you, ma'am, but I saw that pile of cordwood and wondered if y'all here in the house might need it split and stacked."

An older white woman appeared behind her and said, "I'll handle this, Macie." She stepped outside onto the porch. "I'm Amelia Henderson, and we indeed could use some help. You seem like a polite young man. Are you traveling?"

"Yes ma'am, just passing through on the way to Florida for the winter and picking up a little work along the way to pay expenses. If you have an axe and show me where to stack the wood I'll get started."

She turned and said, "Macie, please fetch the axe from the mudroom." She and I went into the yard and she pointed where to build the stack and showed me the stump of what once had been a gigantic oak where I could split the wood.

Mrs. Henderson went back inside just as Macie emerged from a side door carrying an axe and a whetstone. She glowered and said, "No funny business, boy. Troof be told, I be watching you f'om dat parlor winder."

I took off my shirt and sharpened the axe. The wood was seasoned oak. I got to work. My hands had gone soft from those months of dishwashing, and within a half-hour I'd gained some angry blisters. The morning heated up, my unused muscles along with it. The exercise and rhythm of swinging an axe felt good. I stacked the wood using the requisite cross pieces at the ends to keep the pile stable. The job took a couple of hours. I rinsed off my head and upper body using a garden hose, dried off as best I could using my shirt, then pulled it on and knocked at the door. Macie answered. "You done got hit all split and stacked?"

"Yessum. Come see."

She waddled across the porch and eased down the steps sideways holding up the hem of her dress so she didn't trip. She went to the stack and looked it up and down, then nodded. "You done okay. Miz Amelia say to fetch some lemonade, that you might've gained a thirst."

"Yessum, I sure did."

"Well, I'll go fetch hit."

She returned carrying a tray with a pitcher and two glasses. We sat together on a porch swing, the tray on a low table in front of us. I told her it was the best lemonade I'd ever tasted and suggested it came from an old family recipe. She said that it had, her mamaw's, and it was made using fresh lemons, some crushed mint from the garden, and just enough sugar "to hold down the pucker." I laughed, then she did too. She said Miz Amelia had given orders to feed me and asked if I liked egg salad, she'd just made a fresh batch. I said it's one of my favorites, which is true. She picked up the tray and went inside and came out a few minutes later with the refilled pitcher and a thick sandwich and potato chips.

I'd just finished eating when Mrs. Henderson came

out. "Macie says you did a good job on the firewood." When I stood she handed me twenty dollars; I'd been expecting five. "I'm having Macie make you some sandwiches for the road. It'll just be a minute. Of course, if you want to stay a while in Savannah there's lots of work for a handyman. You probably could be employed full time and not leave this neighborhood. All these old houses are falling to pieces and need constant maintenance."

"I sure appreciate the offer, Mrs. Henderson," I said, "but I think I need to get down to Florida in time to find a job for the winter." She said she understood.

Macie came out holding a paper tote bag, the kind with string handles from department stores. I looked inside and saw two thick sandwiches wrapped in waxed paper and a big bag of chips. Two days' food. Macie said, "Hit's local smoked ham sliced thin wid spicy mustard."

I said, "I'm grateful to you both for being kind and generous. Thanks so much." The rest of the afternoon was spent walking around looking at the neighborhoods. It ended in a little park with a circular brick walkway lined with several benches. A fountain bubbled in the center. The place was deserted except for a couple of panhandling pigeons. I decided to sleep there, get to the truck stop for breakfast, and start thumbing the back roads toward Jacksonville. I expected a series of short automobile rides. It would be sheer luck to catch a lift from a trucker going all the way.

Dusk was settling in. I selected a bench and took out a book, *Siddhartha* by Herman Hesse. I'd read it in college. I remembered sitting in the grass on the campus when a girl approached and asked what I was reading. When I showed her the cover she mentioned how cool it was to meet someone reading *Siddhartha*, that hardly anyone even knew about it. We dated a few times, then I got to feeling claustrophobic and stopped contacting her. I was experiencing the usual guilt until she bounced up to me not two weeks later holding the hand of a new boyfriend and telling him I was the guy she met who was reading *Siddhartha*. Evidently, the guilt of romantic breakups isn't universal. In fact, lots of them aren't even romantic to begin with, if the participants take a few minutes to really think about it.

———————

It got too dark to read. The evening was warm. I stretched out with the pack as a pillow. An owl hooted from somewhere nearby, and a few mosquitoes buzzed; otherwise, all was peaceful until someone plopped down on the adjacent bench and turned on a portable radio. I sat up, but details of the intruder were invisible. All I could see were bobbing back-and-forth movements in time to the music. I said, "Excuse me, but could you turn the music down? I'm trying to catch some sleep."

"Whatchu tryin to sleep fo', hit ain't hardly nighttime."

"Tough day," I said.

The volume went down. "That better?"

"Yeah, lots. Thanks."

"No sweat, dude. Hey, wanna buy some drugs?"

I sat up. "What's on sale?"

"Weed and pills."

"What kind of pills? And is the weed mostly stems and oregano?"

"No, man, weed's decent, not great. No buds or nuttin, but hit's been sieved fo' stems and shit. Fo' pills I got uppers, downers, and all arounders. Fo' uppers dey's speed, de usual bennies; fo' downers dey's a new kid onna the block dey calling Big Blue, which is ten milligrams and guaran-damn-teed to fuck you up f'om de get-go. 'Ludes, I got dem too.

"On sale, huh?"

He snorted. "No, man, dat's *y-all's* joke. Cain't give no discounts. I got overhead, you dig? Got to say hit up front, iffen you buy my weed don't fahr hit up here 'cause a beat cop likely to walk by and smell hit."

I took out my flashlight and asked the man to display his wares. "How much?"

"Weed, eight bucks fo' a fo'-finger serving, speed is two caps fo' a buck, 'ludes two bucks a pop. Big Blue jist come on de market, and I still tryin to figger out street value, but fo' you, my man, say, fo' bucks a pop."

I asked his recommendations and whether he ever sampled his products for quality control. "I smoke a little weed to test hit 'cause of de variation. De rest, not so much. Once in a while I gits confused and pop a upper when I meant it to be a downer. I ought to know better, being a professional and all. Speed done makes me loony. I start yellin and runnin around, but I has never hurt nobody." He shrugged. "Where you come from, man? You ain't local, I kin hear hit. You got some kinda hill accent."

"West Virginia."

"I heerd of hit. Where's hit at?"

"North of Georgia some." He nodded.

I said I had twenty dollars in my budget to spend on chemical recreation and went for the speed and quaaludes. Carrying marijuana while thumbing was too risky, and pills were easier to hide if I was stopped by the cops and searched. Business completed I asked if he'd care to join me for supper, that I could offer half a ham sandwich and chips. "Damn right!" he said. "But we need some beers. On me. Liquor store around de corner." I offered to guard his pack. He laughed. "Where I go my inventory go." He wasn't gone fifteen minutes and returned carrying a cold sixer.

I took out one of the sandwiches and gave him half. "Man, dem's thick."

"Smoked ham sliced thin with spicy mustard. Here, have some chips." We pried the caps off two beers and chowed down. He told me his name was Raymond, that he'd been born and raised in Savannah and was seventeen years old. I asked if he was still in school.

"Naw, I quit. School ain't useful. I knows how to count money. What I need is to git outta town and expand de business. I got relatives over to Waycross, but ain't never been over to hit. Cain't afford de bus."

I suggested he could thumb. "You crazy? A Black boy standin roadside, his thumb hangin loose? Wouldn't be ten minutes till a carload of rednecks pulled over and stomped me flat. Nossir, that be a bad idea."

"Do what I do and start at that big truck stop just outside town. Lots of Black drivers pass through those places, and you could get a lift that way. I'll be there myself tomorrow morning looking to get to

Florida." He said he knew the place and which city bus stopped there. I got out the map and showed him that Waycross was maybe a three-hour ride.

"That all? Shee-it, I always thought hit be a long way." The idea excited him, and he said he'd give it a try. He told me his goal was to retire at thirty, buy a big mansion with a swimming pool in the north Georgia mountains, and staff it with naked women. I withheld some private reservations. Who was I to step on someone's dream? At least Raymond had one, which was more than I could say.

We were finishing off the six-pack when the beat cop sauntered up, just as Raymond said he might, and shined his light in our faces. "I seed you around, Black boy. Beat hit. And you, what y'all's bidness here?"

"Just passing through, officer."

"Plan on spending the night on that bench?'

"If it's okay by you."

"Where you from? I got me a good ear for accents, and I figger north Mississippi jist south of Memphis."

"You do have a good ear. Southern West Virginia down near the Kentucky border. Southern Appalachians, we all sound similar."

He nodded. "This here park don't double as a motel."

"Leaving in the morning for Florida. Just here to catch my breath."

"Good. Be careful of the company you keep. Like that Black boy I jist run off. I seed him around a lot and don't trust him. Not 'specially 'cause he's Black, but 'cause he's a smart-ass. Keep that up he'll git my nightstick upside his head. Hear me?"

"Yessir, I surely do. I got the same impression of

him, although I don't think he really means to be that way."

"Maybe, but these kids who quit school oughta be put in the military to learn some respect for a uniform." He tapped his leg with his nightstick. "I'll tell my relief when he comes on at midnight to leave you be."

"Thanks."

"Don't mention hit. Good luck." He turned and walked away a few steps then returned, having something else to say. "We be seeing more of them goddamn Yankee hippies. I was in the Army and don't appreciate their disrespect for the flag."

"I was in the Army too, and I know what you mean."

"That's good to hear. We need all the patriots we kin muster with the shit over in Vietnam. Finish off your beer, police the area, and when morning comes be gone on outta here. The rich bastards in them mansions yonder see any trash in this park and vagrants passed out on the benches, they be on me like flies on shit."

I finished my beer, picked up the trash, and looked around for Raymond, but he had vanished. I popped a 'lude and felt the world drift away.

———

I awoke to find my hands and arms covered in red welts where mosquitoes had feasted. I'd been too stoned to appreciate the experience. My mouth tasted like the contents of an ashtray; my eyeballs seemed to be smeared with petroleum jelly. It was dawn or shortly thereafter. I must have swallowed the 'lude late because I was still stoned and disoriented. I wandered around thinking there must be a bus stop nearby, but even if I found it I had no idea which bus to take. Finally, about nine or so I gave up and hailed a taxi.

At the truck stop I went into the men's room and stuck my head underneath a faucet, scrubbed the gunk from my eyes, and gargled to try and flush away the cotton. The thought of eating or drinking anything was nauseating, but I needed to get straight. I bought a black coffee to go and washed down two bennies while the waitress stood behind the cash register with her hand out waiting to be paid and looking at the ceiling.

The parking lot was bedlam. I waded into the thicket of cops and flashing lights to see what was happening and found myself standing beside two farmers wearing John Deere caps, dusty overalls, and patty hoppers. They were chewing tobacco and looking bored. I asked them what was up. They told me a Black kid had been shot by a trucker, and that the trucker was also Black. The cops were just starting to interview him.

The poor guy was distraught. He was leaning against his cab with his head in his hands and sobbing, shoulders humping up and down. Finally, he got controlled enough to talk. "Scared me half to death. I didn't notice at first dat he was only a kid, but he was yelling crazy shit, like, 'Open de damn do', negro! You owe me a ride, mothafucka!' My winders was rolled down 'cause of the heat, and afo' I could push de lock button he was yanking my do' open. Then he done stuck a hand in his pack. I panicked. Must be a gun or a knife, I thinks to myself. I carry my own gun under the seat fo' protection, and while he done stirred around inside dat pack fo' whatever hit was I fetched hit out and shot him. I gotta tell y'all straight out, dat boy was on something. I mean, he warn't right. I'm so terrible sorry. I never kilt nobody afo'." He started to weep even louder.

I turned away and walked as straight as I could toward the exit, not needing to ask the identity of the victim. I felt vaguely responsible and wondered if he'd confused his pills again.

Chapter 5

I STAGGERED TO THE entrance ramp and flopped in the grass beside it feeling as if all my blood had turned to sludge and was barely oozing through the arteries and veins, the heart pumping in overdrive to overcome the friction. Somewhere in the distance a big rig was honking, but when I looked up it was idling directly beside me, a colossal red machine exhaling black exhaust. The driver leaned over and rolled down the window, then opened the door. He was so high up I could see just his head. "Stand back and let me get a look at you," he shouted. "I can tell lots by how a feller looks and if I want him riding shotgun." I could barely make out the words above the rough rumble and growl of his rig and hissing of its Jake Brake system.

I stood uncertainly and stepped back so he got a full view, spread my arms, and turned a three-sixty.

"Where you from?"

After a few seconds too long I said West Virginia.

"You're a little fucked up, boy." Then he nodded. "Get in."

I put a foot on the step and swung inside. I said, "Thanks, mister," and stuck the pack between my feet. My head seemed unbalanced and wouldn't stay upright. Keeping it from rolling side to side seemed impossible no matter how hard I focused.

The driver ignored it and said, "How far you aim to go?"

"Key West."

"You mean Queer West? I been there. Packs of queers everywhere, walking around holding hands like they was normal and it's the rest of us who's fucked up." He turned and looked in the side mirror and upshifted as we merged onto the road, then gave me a sideways glance. "If you reach under your seat you'll find a bottle of Jack Daniel's. Help yourself to a slug, then pass it over. Maybe it'll straighten you out some. That is, if it ain't too early in the day for you." I looked over at him, and he looked back. The difference was that I saw two of him, one superimposed and slightly off-center of the other. He flashed two smiles that had no teeth behind either. Over top of them were four piggy little blue eyes. The smiles didn't look especially friendly, and the eyes reflected no warmth or humor.

I did as he said and unscrewed the cap. It felt smooth going down, a cloud above the usual rotgut I was used to. I nodded in appreciation and handed him the bottle. He'd been right: I did feel a little better, or at least I told myself that.

"Say, hey!" He jabbed the bottle at the ceiling of

the cab. "I could use some relief podner." Again, he gave me that curious sideways glance more watchful than warm.

"I ain't licensed to drive a rig like this," I said, snapping back my head as I said it. Something still wasn't right. Either my equilibrium or the road was filled with potholes. We were on a two-lane county road, I hoped headed south. He still hadn't mentioned his destination.

"I didn't mean that. I'll say it right out. I got a twenty-dollar bill stuck down the front of my jeans, a heap of dough for somebody like you. It's all yours, but you'll have to bob for it."

I guess I looked as stupid and broke as I felt. He was right that it was a lot of dough for those times and guys like me. I looked at him in focus for the first time. He was a jelly-belly, the bottom of the steering wheel slipping neatly between his roll and belt buckle, and he smelled like a goat, not that I probably smelled any better. "Take it somewhere else," I said, and accepted the bottle he held out.

"Suit yourself," he said, and started struggling with the zipper of his fly. I watched furtively as he pulled out his dick, and after spitting in his left palm, started yanking on it.

I took another swig then screwed the cap on and tried looking out the passenger window but the scene bouncing past in a blur made me dizzy and slightly nauseous. I leaned my head back and closed my eyes. The drug fog was nowhere near dissipating, the more familiar alcohol buzz now an incipient presence.

He said, "Open that glovebox and reach out the

magazine." It was the April issue of *Playboy*. "Go to the centerfold and tear it out, the whole spread, both pages, and have a good look. Now, ain't that a purty sight? Bet you'd like some of it." Once again that cold, watchful look my way. "Hand it over." Still working his left hand, he pinned the photo to the top of the steering wheel with his right and began flicking glances between it and the highway ahead. The speedometer needle was quivering on the seventy mark. I had no idea what we were hauling, but hoped it was soft and squishy considering the likelihood it could land on top of us.

The left hand sped up, and suddenly he squashed the photo over his member. "You steer!" His eyes rolled back in his head, and he started huffing, "Oh God! Oh my God!" and shot into the paper now wrapped around his dick and which he held in place with both hands. The truck was driving itself. My drug high was still at the stage where very real Tinker Bells the size of lightning bugs flashed all around, their movements now restrained somewhat by the whiskey.

We were drifting toward the shoulder. The steering mechanism had a sluggish response, requiring more forceful tugs on the wheel than I'd anticipated. I twisted in the seat, grabbed the wheel in my right hand, and torqued it counter-clockwise, scarcely discerning the feeble feedback. The situation was slipping out of control. I sensed an impending jackknife and the kinds of bad shit that come afterward, notably dismemberment and death. I heard someone with my voice but outside myself yelling, "Grab the goddamn wheel!" We were headed straight at an oncoming car, its driver leaning on the horn. My companion snapped the steering wheel from me and guided us back into our lane with a second to spare, just as the car slipped past, horn still blaring and leaving behind its Doppler effect to fill in the distance.

A minute later when we were again cruising on even keel he pushed the sticky wad of paper toward me. "Throw this away."

"Throw it away yourself," I said. I wasn't about to touch it.

Chapter 6

—◆◆—

WE HAD NOTHING MORE to say to each other, and I was content to lie back and gradually recover. We pulled into a truck stop on the north side of Jacksonville and got out. As we were walking toward the diner he said, "See you around. . .honey." I went straight to the men's room and bought a black coffee to go, then stood at the exit ramp sipping it and eating half of Macie's second ham sandwich. From there the trip was uneventful. In three or maybe four lifts, I don't recall exactly, I was in Homestead south of Miami near the start of the Florida Keys and the Overseas Highway to Key West.

A local guy driving a pickup dropped me at a 7-11 after a short ride and said it was a good spot to hitch. I went inside and bought a Coke, and while I was drinking it a Pepsi delivery truck pulled up. The driver struggled with a hand truck holding several cases. I ran to hold the door. He said, "Thanks, man. You should be drinking Pepsi," and laughed. I asked if he was going south to the Keys, and he said, yeah, all the way to the end dropping Pepsi at various stops along the way. I asked for a lift, and he said, sure, long as you don't mind helping me unload. I said I didn't mind at all. We introduced ourselves and shook. He said he really wasn't allowed to carry passengers because of company insurance regulations, but what the hell.

I told him my plan to get a job, probably in Key West, the island having the biggest population. I figured that meant more job opportunities. I said I could do a number of things, from auto mechanics to dishwashing and asked his opinion of where to start looking. He explained that the term "conch" in local jargon refers to someone who's a permanent resident of the Florida Keys. He described "conchs" as mostly peaceful, but independent and irreverent. Conchs overran Key West. In fact, Key West was known unofficially as the Conch Republic and even had a flag. He said that the staff and clientele at his last stop instantiated the "conch" breed. He described it as a funky resort on the Atlantic Ocean a couple of blocks from the southernmost point in the United States. Ocean Shores Resort was its name. It catered mainly to gays and lesbians, who came to vacation from all over the world, although everyone was welcome. The bar and pool were clothes-optional. The premises boasted a fully stocked liquor store and a diner named, "Wait for it," he said, "Diner Shores. No shit, that's its name." This being the slack season I might enjoy staying there while looking for employment. It seemed like a reasonable idea.

I stepped into the air-conditioned office. Straight ahead was the reception desk; actually, a counter with a desk underneath. Two guys with their arms wrapped around each other's waist stood before it, their backs to me. They were accompanied by a small dog on a leash. The phone rang and the guy behind the counter answered: "Hello, Ocean Shores Resort and Fun House. How may I help you? Hold please." He said to me, "Have a seat, sweetie. Where are you coming from?"

"New York," I said.

"Oh my, well, I have a call on hold, and these gentlemen are in front of you. I'll be with you in a Key West minute. That's the opposite of a New York minute, meaning you might be here all day." He got back on the phone and gave out some room prices, then hung up.

One of the two guys said, "You allow dogs, right?"

"Yes, sweetie, but you're responsible for any damage it does. If it destroys an expensive object. . .wait, that's impossible. I'd know you stole it from the Holiday Inn. Okay, one bed or two? Never mind, stupid question. I trust you won't be smuggling any women into your room. Sorry, I don't want to come across as heterophobic. Some of my best friends are women, but I still wouldn't want them to touch me." He grimaced.

The phone rang. The clerk answered it and went into listening mode. He put a hand over the mouthpiece and whispered, "Give me a moment, sweeties." When it was his turn to speak he said, "I won't stand for it, you little faggot bitch," and slammed down the receiver. "Pardon me," he said, "but people can be so goddamn fucking rude. And the language!" He shook his head in disgust.

"This is slack season, and we have several choices available at reduced prices, he said." He came out from behind the counter and went to a graphic taped to the wall. We gathered around. It had descriptions and maps of all the rooms, which he called "suites" because they included, in various combinations, king – or queen-sized beds, two double beds, small refrigerators, coffee makers, telephone, and TV. The guys made their choice. He handed them a key and directed them to turn left and follow the sidewalk.

After they had gone he looked me up and down. "If you're on a budget, and you look like you are," he said primly, "then I'd recommend our least expensive suite, which has a single queen bed. It doesn't come with a refrigerator." He turned and blinked myopically through spectacles so thick they magnified his eyes to the size of huge marbles.

I took it, saying I didn't know how many nights I'd be staying, that I would be looking for employment. We introduced ourselves. He said he was the manager and his name was Joseph, but he preferred Josephine, or just Josie. He asked what sort of work I did. I described myself as a handyman.

"How 'handsy' are you?"

"It's *handy*."

"Damn," he said, and laughed. "Another episode in my sad life of chronic rejections. Oh well, onward and upward. Tell me more."

I explained that I could fix nearly anything: auto

engines, some appliances, minor electrical and plumbing issues, that I also had carpentry, painting, tiling, and drywalling skills. Whatever needed doing. Recently, I said, I had been working in Coney Island as a dishwasher but considered that just a stop-gap gig until something more lucrative came along, and I'd come to Key West because I was weary of cold winters. I said I repaired and reglazed windows, but didn't wash them.

Josie said that Ocean Shores had seventy-two suites. Something was always breaking. And some of the guests are so thoughtless. . . .He rolled his marble-sized eyes. "Of course, we charge them for any damage, but the stuff still needs fixing after they leave. I'm looking for an all-around handyman. Tell me your requirements."

"First, show me your tools."

He wiggled his eyebrows. "You *really* want to see them?"

"Uh, like the hammers and saws and such."

He sighed. "How boring, but follow me."

We stepped outside. He sashayed down the sidewalk, me tagging along, and opened the door to a large storeroom in disarray. Junk was everywhere. "This is it, sweetie." The tool collection comprised some screwdrivers, a hammer, and a jar of assorted nails with a rusty lid.

"How have you been getting stuff fixed?" I said.

"Piecemeal. For plumbing I call a plumber. For electrical, an electrician. It's expensive as hell, and sometimes they don't show up for days. It's driving me bonkers."

"Well, I can't fix anything without tools. If I accept

the job you'll need to open your wallet, keeping in mind that every job taken care of in-house saves the cost of a licensed tradesman, and, I hope, gets done in a timely way. In the end you'll come out ahead."

We went back to the office and discussed terms of employment. I needed a starting budget for tools. Job one, I said, was mucking out the storeroom, tossing out the useless stuff, then installing a lock on the door and making some of the space into a workroom. As for myself, I needed free housing. The most reasonable and cost-effective for the resort would be one of the queen efficiencies. These had air-conditioning, ceiling fan, bathroom with shower, refrigerator, coffee maker, TV, and phone. I saw that a hotplate wasn't included, but I needed one so I could prepare some simple meals occasionally to save money. I said I'd reimburse the resort for long-distance calls. This was a red herring as a negotiating ploy because I knew there wouldn't be many, maybe none. The suite must come with the usual daily maid service and include my personal laundry. I also wanted health insurance in case I fell off a ladder, an employee discount to eat at Diner Shores, and the bar to lay a few complimentary drinks on me now and then, the number of which would be up to me. I wasn't a barfly, I assured him, and wouldn't take advantage, although an ice-cold beer on a hot day sure provided inspiration to work harder. Finally, I needed one day a week off. It would be at my choosing and vary depend-ing on workload. Otherwise, I'd be on call. As for salary, a hundred and a quarter a week would be sufficient, and that's a discount because of the other amenities.

Josie hadn't said anything until then. At the

mention of salary he screamed and jumped out of his chair. *"What?* Are you out of your fucking mind? That's outrageous. I won't go higher than a hundred-ten."

"A hundred-fifteen," I countered.

He rubbed his chin. "Okay. As Mother always told me, if you're going to be a whore, be an expensive one. I'll put you on the payroll starting today and show you to your suite."

I called for a dumpster. It took two days to empty the storeroom. There were broken chaises and chairs from the bar and pool deck, nearly everything beyond repair. This is what happens when people who can't fix things save such objects in the mistaken belief they possess actual value and that in the future maybe someone else can. Then the stuff gets shoved to the back as other stuff, equally useless, is tossed into the room: for example, a shovel with a broken handle, an unsalvageable weed whacker out of string, moldy tablecloths. . . .Hardly anything was worth repairing, including the window air-conditioner, now a condominium for wasps. I added a replacement to my growing list of tools and supplies. I planned to clear some of the space for a work area, and I didn't intend to sweat unduly.

Josie gave me a street map of Key West. I got out the phone book and marked the addresses of the nearest stores for auto supplies, tools, hardware, and lumber. I had Josie call the managers in advance to set up accounts. Soon it was time to go shopping. Well, almost. The resort's van—a dented, rusting Ford—was dead. I added some essential auto repair tools to my shopping list.

Ida, one of the bartenders, had a car and drove me to the auto supplies store for a new battery, but after putting it in place the engine kept stalling, sign of a bad ignition switch. Back to the store. Once the damn thing was running there was a carburetor issue requiring a third trip for a carburetor kit. A faulty carburetor is in certain respects similar to a stammerer. You turn the key and instead of the engine speaking smoothly and clearly it hiccups, gasps and groans, hems and haws, coughs and sneezes, trying desperately to expel a suitably responsive sound. Ida took these inconveniences in good humor, and we got acquainted. She was a lesbian from Philadelphia, about six-feet-two, and had been at Ocean Shores for four years. The other bartender was a gay guy named Junior, who was at least a foot shorter. I met him later. Together, they were a comedy team and kept the customers laughing and buying drinks, and, of course, pushing tips their way.

Reviving the van, including oiling the door hinges and tuning it up, took two days. The tires were cracking from dry rot. I drove to a tire store and had four cheap replacements installed. It still needed an oil change and lube, which I had done at a gas station. Josie was impressed. He came out of the office and said the van hadn't been used in weeks because the staff couldn't start it, and the one time it did start the engine stalled. He had been nervous about having it towed to a garage, wary of what the repair bill might be. I told him he'd already saved hundreds, and I would keep fixing what was reasonable considering the resort's lack of tools and auto repair facilities.

Chapter 7

———••———

FALL SLID INTO WINTER, and the weather was mostly beautiful. I was thinking more and more about the crew at Catalano's and missing them. Everyone there had been really good to me. Stupid, I know, but it's how I was feeling. So, I bought a postcard and a stamp in the office and addressed it to the restaurant. On the front was a doctored photograph of a girl in a bikini kneeling on a beach beside a palm tree. She's looking over her shoulder smiling into the camera while an alligator with its mouth open seems about to bite her ass. It said VISIT FLORIDA! I wrote that Key West is great and gave the address and phone number where I was working.

About a week later Josie handed me one of those messages you tear off a pad saying you missed a call. On it Josie had written Angel's name and a return phone number I recognized as Catalano's. After knocking off work that day I went to my room and called him. Renato answered and said it was good hearing from me. I had to tell him all I was doing, how the weather was in Florida, and so on, then he went to get Angel, and when he got on I had to start over. I finally said this call is long-distance and costing me a fortune, but thanks for phoning.

He said, "I forgot to tell youse why I called. Catalano's is gonna close a whole month for a makeover. This ain't never happened before, like, in fifty years or whatever. But it's about time. The place, as youse knows, is a dump on close inspection, or even not so close. The floors need refinishing, the kitchen equipment is old and crappy. Same wit the furniture in the dining area and banquet room. The only stuff the owners plan on keeping is them photos on the walls, youse remember, shots of *capos* and wiseguys sitting around the table in the banquet room, fat cigars stuck in their faces, and the Rat Pack leaning over them flashing fish-eating grins. That stuff. So, me and Willie and Lenny, we're coming down to visit youse and get suntans, and we're bringing Hercules, who's never went on vacation in his life. So, book us some rooms at that place."

"It's tight," I said. "Rooms are booked sometimes a year in advance. Give me the exact dates, 'cause once y'all are penciled in there's no changing anything."

"I'll get back in a day or so," Angel said, and hung up.

He phoned the next day and said he'd hold, so Josie came and found me. "The middle of April is when we're coming down. Catalano's will be closed then. Willie and Lenny want separate suites, good ones. Hercules and me ain't as flush. We'll bunk together, just separate beds. Phone me back wit details when it's set. I'm the de facto travel agent in this enterprise. Next I gotta do plane reservations and rental car. What a pain in the ass, but if I leave the planning to them mooks Willie and Lenny it's sure to get fucked up."

I went to Josie. He looked at the calendar. "Christ, mid-April is Easter, Spring Break. We're booked solid. And they want the weeks before and after Easter?"

"This is really, really important," I said. "These are my best friends. I doubt if they even know it'll be Easter, and they probably never heard of Spring Break. They need two king suites oceanside and a double-bed standard, the one with two beds. Can't you do something?"

He looked at his April bookings. "King suites are out of the question, but maybe not queens. Let's see. . . .Speaking of queens oceanside, I can cancel out a pair of pansies from Minneapolis. They're whiners, always bitching about maid service or the wait staff in the diner, whatever. I'll tell them I accidentally double-booked. Another queen oceanside. . . ." He expelled air through his teeth and turned pages. "Aha! I have two fairies from Atlanta booked through those days. Don't know them. It's a first-time reservation on a referral. They're fixated on the tea dances. They say they're bringing their cat, and I fucking hate cats. I'll tell them the same thing. The double-bed standard is no problem, just a couple of college boys. I'll say the suite is being renovated and blow them off. Figuratively speaking, of course." He looked at me and grinned.

I said, "Thanks, Josie. I can't tell you how much I appreciate this."

He said, "You're welcome, but I'm running late."

He looked at his watch. "Got to spackle the face and paint the eyebrows before Arnold arrives. We have a dinner date and maybe something extra special for dessert." He wiggled his eyebrows, then sighed. "Straight men have life so easy. Just throw on any old thing and walk out the door."

———————

The Christmas season arrived, and the denizens of Key West went crazy over decorating their domiciles and businesses. Streetlamps were draped in tinsel and plastic wreaths, and a sparkling, tawdry universe came into existence under a galaxy of tinfoil stars and iridescent quarter-moons.

Josie was in high spirits, proclaiming it his favorite time of year. He trundled around the office hanging Christmas stuff and had me drag an artificial spruce out of the storeroom where I had stashed it behind everything else figuring it would never be used. It was easily seven feet tall and four feet wide, and when I'd been cleaning out the place a few months previously and asked Josie if I could toss it he screamed, "Over my gay dead body!" It and several boxes of ornaments had made the cut, and now the staff was happily putting it all to use.

Christmas, like birthdays, had never been a big deal in my life, and I found getting into the spirit of the season somewhat awkward. It didn't take me long to learn that I must have been the only person around with this attitude. I felt self-conscious replying in a lilting voice, "Merry Christmas to you too!" when someone said Merry Christmas to me. I can understand how people with families or even just a significant other might think differently, although most of the residents I'd met either lived alone or with roommates of no relation. There were many resident couples in Key West, of course, gay and straight, but they and I rarely interacted except to say hello in the bar or diner.

I didn't attend any regular events staged by the resort except an occasional "Thursday Night Under the Stars" when movies were shown. Judy Garland flicks were especially popular. For some reason they cause gay men to weep unashamedly. Same with *Sunset Boulevard*. I never did catch the connection, but at critical moments the sobbing nearly drowned out the dialogue and background music. For these events the parking lot was cleared beforehand. We set up a movie screen and provided seating using outdoor furniture dragged over from the pool area, although people often brought their own chairs. Drinks and popcorn were sold.

Sunday nights from seven to eleven featured the outdoor "tea dance," formally known as "Tea by the Sea." I'm not much for dancing and never actually attended, although I occasionally stopped in my rounds for a few minutes to watch the participants and listen to the band.

The resort was about half filled by the twenty-fourth. Josie had posted a notice that the diner and bar would close early Christmas Eve and not reopen until the day after Christmas to allow the staff time off. Christmas Eve arrived, and Josie organized a low-key staff party in the empty bar starting around seven. Arnold, his lover, was in Virginia spending Christmas with relatives. The maids and gardeners didn't show, nor did any of the Diner Shores staff or the parttime handyman assistant I had finally browbeaten Josie into hiring, not after considerable whining and stonewalling. I had finally put the matter to him realistically, explaining that two could paint twice as fast as one, and if he wanted the rooms repainted on his unrealistic schedule, plus all the other tasks, then I needed help. Also, this guy knew some plumbing and wiring and could even lay bathroom tile. He was actually a bargain, costing the resort just fifty cents an hour above minimum wage. I didn't expect to keep him long, considering his skills nearly matched my own, minus the auto mechanics.

We gathered at the bar and at Josie's instigation played a game of tell-all on ourselves. In attendance were Josie, Ida, Junior, Jerry, and me. Jerry was a long-time Key West resident and gadfly. Nobody I knew considered him a friend, at best an acquaintance, a gay man who lived alone, hung out at the bar ogling the college boys, and rarely missed the special events. He owned a little junk shop and referred to himself as an "antiques dealer."

Frankly, Jerry was a minor annoyance and usually was in a sour mood, but Josie explained to us before he arrived that we should feel sorry for him, it being Christmas Eve and him home alone, that tonight was a time to be kind to one another and think only happy thoughts. He described Jerry as one of those people who can never become attached to anyone. Jerry, he reminded us, had originally been a switch-hitter before deciding he preferred women. However, women he took up with told him he drank too much, didn't earn enough money, cheated on them, and that, in general, he was an all-around shithead. At that point he switched to men, and know what? Same deal.

To stimulate us in the direction of charitable Christian thoughts Josie asked Ida to put some upbeat music on the stereo, not traditional Christmas season stuff, but light and pleasant. Junior offered to tend bar. We started by downing a couple of shots of our favorite liquor. No reason to hold back, considering the cost of the night's festivities were on the house, and we had tomorrow to sleep off our hangovers.

"Okay, listen up," Josie said. "The subject of this evening's tell-all is about the love of your life. I'll go first to set the example. The rules are, we have to be truthful and promise not to leave out important details. No shirking. Warts and all, even tears, okay? This is Christmas Eve." He turned and gazed dreamily in the direction of the ocean.

"His name was Edwardo. I'd recently stepped warily out of the closet and was still trying to convince myself I didn't care what people think of gays. I could take it. Not all God's chilluns is alike, I said to me, so fuck it. He and I met on the Nantucket ferry out of Woods Hole, Massachusetts. How appropriate, eh? Two fairies meet on a ferry." He chuckled.

"I was standing at the stern rail gazing absently down at the prop wash and looking forward to sunning at the beach. It was late May and time to get working on my tan. I was assistant manager of a motel in Falmouth on Cape Cod. It felt good, getting away from people before the summer tourist season hit fully on.

Nothing to do for two days except lie in the sun, read, and enjoy some quiet meals alone. Boy, was I wrong!

"Suddenly, my reverie was interrupted by someone approaching, and then he was standing beside me. I didn't dare look, so I kept staring at the prop wash, glancing up furtively at the mob of gulls that always follows the big boats as they leave port. I had been thinking momentarily of the frenzy of that prop wash as my life's metaphor. We're all seeking love even if we don't consciously realize it. There was my life roiling below: turbulent, directionless, murky, leveling out behind into a calmer wake. Was this what the future held? Stability eventually attenuating into death after the last of the motion dissipated and my molecules, now devoid of personal identity, blended into the impersonal sea around? Sorry for the digression. Shit, I think I'm tipsy.

"Anyway, there he was. I couldn't keep avoiding him forever, could I? So, I glanced over. He was dark-complexioned and had a slim build, his eyes so deep brown they were almost black. 'Hi,' he said, and smiled. 'You are going to Nantuc, uh Nantuc. . . .'

"To Nantucket, yes, and I suppose you are too.

"'Yes, yes. I am staying Nan, Nan, Nantucket.' We both laughed. 'I have hard time with that word, no? I need, how you say, practice.' I couldn't unlock my eyes from his. It's as if I was paralyzed, or trapped in one of those science fiction time warps. Finally, I asked him where he was from.

"'From where I am? Colombia. I am from Bogotá.' It struck me as so cute, the struggle he was going through just to communicate with me. I felt special to be the object of all that effort. Then he said something in Spanish I didn't understand. Later he wrote it down so I could remember. He said *Admiro tu tresero*, but there on the boat I had no clue. I said, 'What?'

"Then he said, '*Me gusta tu tresero*.'

"Later, he wrote that down too. At the time all I could think to say was, 'Well, if you say so. I'll believe anything you tell me.' Then the most romantic thing happened. I held out my hand to introduce myself, and he got down on one knee and kissed it. Goodness, holy fuck! I almost fainted! No one had ever done that before, nor after, I might add. I've held out my hand to attractive men hundreds of times since, and all they ever do is shake it. How dull. Oh god, is chivalry really dead?

"Edwardo stood and leaned an elbow on the rail. It was such a sexy pose I was completely captivated. Then came, 'Ah, hell, I'm not Colombian but my parents are. I was born and raised in Boston,' and he started to laugh. 'I thought I'd try this pickup line. Think it'd work?' Naturally, I didn't know whether to be charmed or offended until he added, 'You really do have a great ass, and I do truly admire it.'

"I must have turned crimson. Well, he was the one. I knew instantly. Yep, I said to myself, you are the one. We went straight to the hotel, checked into my room, and barely got out of bed for two days and three nights. If I'd ever wondered how a virgin bride feels on waking up the morning after her wedding night, now I knew. Not that I was virgin, oh my no. I'd sown my wild oats, not that anything ever germinated, not from sex with men. But I certainly was sore that morning, and when I opened my eyes there was Edwardo, bless his heart, gazing softly at me and wanting more ass.

"I had to leave, but he kept the room and stayed. I gave him my phone number. He claimed not to have a phone because he was moving. Of course, he never called." Josie teared up. I put my arm around him and let him snuffle on my shoulder.

After a minute or so he pulled away. He took off his glasses and wiped his eyes. "Okay, your turn, sweetie. You have a tough act to follow."

I told them about meeting Julie and Amy by accident on the boardwalk in Coney Island when Amy, who was three, grabbed my leg and called me daddy. I described her big blue eyes and Julie's, how we walked along talking with Amy falling asleep in my arms, how Amy had a way of penetrating directly into my being and made me feel self-conscious and small and a loser. I said I reckoned it was love on my part because I had not sensed those particular feelings of closeness before or after. I talked about fixing things in their apartment and bringing over dinners from Catalano's and spending nights with them, a welcome break from the hotel where Angel and I shared a room.

I was drunk, slurring words and aware of throwing light on these feelings for the first time; in fact, I had never before organized and articulated them even to myself, trying instead to keep Julie and Amy sealed away in some dark closet of memory while pretending they had never existed and were better off wherever they were. Or so I rationalized, and it was working to some extent until Josie caught me up in his tell-all game. My deepest, most private thoughts and feelings suddenly lay on the surface for everyone to criticize. And it wasn't long in coming.

Ida lit into me. "You left this fine woman and her treasure of a daughter without saying goodbye?" She was incredulous. "You shit of a human being! I'd like to string you up by the balls!"

I stared down at my empty glass. Without looking up I wiggled it for Junior to refill.

"You're such a loser!"

I look sideways at her and acceded. "You're right. I just couldn't accept the responsibility. They say you can't run away from your problems, but I'm proof that you can sometimes run away from the results." And then I was weeping and Josie was hugging me and saying, "There, there, sweetie, it's okay." But it wasn't.

What a night. Junior was the next sacrifice. He said he had a congenital weakness that wasn't his fault. Put simply, he fell in love with every man who had sex with him. He qualified this by insisting he wasn't promiscuous in the true sense. In other words, he never went looking for one-night stands or casual quickies. It was just that he couldn't help feeling emotional attachments to his lovers.

"No matter how you rationalize such behavior, you're still a *whore*," Jerry said.

"Ida turned on him. Now, that's really unkind, you arrant cocksucker! You don't know Junior at all, and there you go cutting him down, an ugly little pansy like yourself."

Jerry said, "Listen, dyke, I don't have to take shit from the likes of you. Get outta my face."

Josie said, "People, *people*! Both of you, please shut

the fuck up. Junior, fill their glasses. What would the newborn baby Jesus say if he overheard this conversation? Gracious! Him so innocent in his swaddling clothes, waiting patiently with Mary and Joseph for the three wise men."

"He wouldn't say anything," Ida said. "He was just a baby, and everyone in the stable—the humans, at least—only spoke Aramaic."

I'd been mostly silent, as is my nature, except for the recent disquisition prompted by Josie. However, that changed in an instant after Josie said, "I'm humbled and honored on this night to have been named for one of Christ's parents."

"Which one?" I said. It sent us into howls of laughter that didn't subside for a full couple of minutes.

Then Josie caught his breath. "Junior, refills please."

But Junior's hands were busy wiping his eyes. "And that's not all," he managed to say between gulps of air. "I look in the mirror every morning and notice that my ass is sagging, and I'm getting lines around my eyes. I'm growing old, and there nothing more pathetic than an aging faggot." He added with malice, "Ask Jerry how it feels!"

Josie the peacemaker said, "That's not true, Junior. What are you, thirty? I think you have a darling ass. Everyone who agrees please join me in a round of applause for Junior's tight little ass." Junior offered a painful smile, and everyone except Jerry clapped and cheered.

"Okay," said Josie the emcee. "Your turn to bat, Ida. God, I love sports metaphors. They make me feel so. . .so masculine!"

"Josie, you prick. You know I hate talking about myself. I'd much rather jeer at other people's flaws and then offer appropriate insults. But since you asked, well, she was a coed I met here at the bar two years back at Spring Break. Talk about a cute ass! I couldn't take my eyes off it, but of course neither could the college so-called studs strutting around in their tank tops and swimsuits, when they weren't buck naked displaying their "mammalinity." Faulkner used that word in *Requiem for a Nun*. He must have made it up because it isn't in the dictionary. Anyhow, Junior says there's nothing uglier than an old faggot, well, he's wrong. The ugliest thing is a man's penis and scrotum. I look at a set of those too long and feel like puking in my mouth a little.

"So, this chick, as I said, was exceedingly popular with all the college bozos hanging out at the bar yearning to get laid. I watched her for the first two days, how she was fending them off and seemed to be looking around for an upgrade, so I made my move. I asked her name, which was Laurie. She was twenty, a junior at LSU in Baton Rouge. I told her I'd gone to Swarthmore in Philly and was from Pennsylvania. Turned out, she was too, Allentown. We'd made that connection, so I pushed on, asking if she'd picked out any particular dude for a good time. She said no, that actually they disgusted her the way they were so egotistical and aggressive, thinking their shit didn't stink and they were God's gift, and so forth. Naturally, I agreed and asked if she might like to join me for a quiet drink at noon the next day, and she accepted.

"My compadre Junior covered me at opening bell.

I met Laurie in the office at noon, as we'd agreed, and took her for lunch and drinks to La Te Da. She loved the setting, and I told her about the drag shows and said I'd be happy to accompany her to one.

"On a bold chance because Laurie had not flashed any signals about liking women I reached under the table and put my hand on her knee. Brazen and risky, I know, but that was the test: would she hold it or slap it away? Diagnose the moment wrong and you're toast. Oh well, I thought, as the trite but true dictum goes, nothing ventured, nothing gained. She didn't do either, but acted like it wasn't happening. In fact, I was looking into her eyes at the moment. Her pupils hadn't changed size, and she didn't blink. Weird, I thought, to receive no response, so I moved my hand a little higher. That was when she started to stroke it, and I knew I was in.

"She had a room to herself at Ocean Shores, and after drinking several margaritas and getting tipsy we went there and spent the rest of the afternoon. Eventually, I had to go to work, but promised to come see her after the bar closed. I clued Junior to the situation, and he said to go ahead and split early, that he could handle the crowd alone.

"God, I fell in love like never before. Like, all the way, crazy head over heels and all that platitudinous horseshit. I was wild for all of her and licked her like a lollipop. She was crazy mostly for my tongue. We couldn't keep our hands off one another, but it was even deeper. We had so much in common. I'd been a comparative lit major at Swarthmore, and that was her major at LSU. When we weren't making love we talked about our favorite books, and lots of them were the same. Josie, you remember when I asked for a couple of extra days off now and then? It's when I was flying up to Baton Rouge to see Laurie. Junior knew it, but I didn't want my life to be other people's business, know what I mean?"

"I understand, sweetie," Josie said.

"Goddammit, don't call me that! Aw, I forgot. You call everybody that." She gave him a hug.

"It couldn't last. Neither of us was the type to settle down and play house. Anyhow, we just sort of drifted apart. She went to grad school at Ohio State, and I, well, stayed right here pouring drinks for the rest of the freaks, present company included. But I'll never forget Laurie, and I hope it all worked out for her." She set down her glass and started to cry. "You've never seen me cry before, but I can't help it. The first one of you faggots who calls me a pussy is getting his ass stomped." Junior came around the bar, and he, Josie, and I squeezed her tight.

When a respectful minute or two had gone by and we had stopped patting and comforting Ida, Josie said, "Well, Jerry. Your turn in the barrel."

"I'm not playing this silly game," he said haughtily. He stood to leave, then turned and said, "You're nothing but a bunch of maudlin queers."

As he left Josie put his hand over his mouth feigning shock. "Oh my! Somebody remind me to delete Jerry's name from my Christmas card list. Well, fellow queers, if the shoe fits, how's about another libation? Who's in favor of dumping the maudlin part and celebrate just being queer?" He raised his glass.

"What about me?" I said.

"And Junior," Josie said, "When you pour, please include our token straight here." He clapped me on the shoulder."

A couple of days later Ida caught up with me and apologized. "I'm sorry about Christmas Eve. I'm a shit too when it comes to relationships. In the end I always run away. Who the hell am I to criticize anyone? We're all shits. Stop by the bar for a cold one when you knock off." She gave me a hug that left me convinced some of my chest cartilage had been rearranged.

––––––––––

Shortly after the new year I reported to Josie that my room hadn't been cleaned in a week, and the dirty laundry was piling up.

"Oh good Christ, not again," he said.

"Have you looked into the laundry room lately?"

"I try not to."

"All that dirty laundry is unhygienic. Ever had the crabs?"

That got his attention. He looked up from his desk. "Of course not!"

"Well, I have," I lied.

"Why am I not surprised."

"Know what would happen for business if a guest caught a case and word got out?"

"Please!" He grabbed his head in both hands.

"Let's not let that happen," I said. "Who trains and supervises the maids?"

"I do. . .sort of. I pay them to clean and do laundry, but I don't follow them around." He added caustically,

"I'm a little busy, you know."

"I know, but maybe you should, at least until they realize they're being monitored."

"Shit, I'm really, really busy. Seriously. Would you do it?"

"I know you're under a lot of pressure, and I want to help. I'll do it for another twenty bucks a week."

He sighed. "You've got me by the scrotum, dammit. Okay."

"For starters we need to hire a fourth maid. There's too much work for three. What are the names of those we have so I can go talk to them?"

"Beats me."

I bought a pair of four-wheeled, double-shelved, stainless steel carts. The maids had been carrying laundry and supplies back and forth in their arms and in buckets, which clearly was inefficient. I went to their supply closet and took inventory then went into vacant suites of the different categories to assess how many sheets of appropriate size, pillow cases, towels, and facecloths were used daily, ditto the soap, shampoo, and toilet paper. It was a simple matter to sum the items and estimate how many were dispensed weekly, plus a five percent cushion for loss, waste, and theft. I inventoried the cleaning supplies and phoned the supplier to reset the weekly delivery schedule, bought clipboards and pencils, and ran off a stack of mimeographed check sheets. When the infrastructure was in place I went in search of the maids and found them loafing in the laundry room surrounded by piles of dirty laundry. I explained there was a new sheriff in town, and efficiency was now required. I emphasized that I expected to be taken seriously. They looked at me, jabbered a moment to one another in Haitian French, and convulsed into giggles.

We did a series of practice runs, entering a room and leaving a cart loaded with clean washables and supplies parked outside the door. Inside, we changed the bedclothes together, cleaned the sink and shower, vacuumed and mopped the floors, and replaced the used towels and facecloths with clean ones. We checked the supplies of disposable items and afterward practiced using the check sheet. There would be two maids per room, and a room wasn't declared cleaned until all items had been marked off. I clocked how long it took to service each category of suite and padded the average time by twenty percent for sloughing off.

Afterward, the washables needed laundering. Again, we ran through the procedure with me keeping time. I thought, why wait until the rooms had been cleaned to start on the laundry? Maid and laundry services, including guest laundry, could be performed simultaneously. I laid this out for Josie, who admitted that the most common gripe from the guests was poor maid service and that something needed to be done. Good, I told him, because we need six maids total, four to clean the rooms and two working the laundry room. We would rotate them. I made a schedule substituting numbers for names and showed him how it worked. He screamed about the inconvenience of having more personnel added to his workload. He cursed and whined about the cost. In the end he agreed grudgingly but later endorsed the new system enthusiastically when it produced results, and he started receiving compliments from the guests.

One night partly from boredom I got drunk in a bar near the resort and started coming down with a case of the sorries. Poor me. I didn't have anyone to love and love me back. The world is such a lonely place. You know the helping of bullshit we sometimes serve ourselves, even realizing at the time it's bullshit but for reasons of weakness and stupidity let it play out anyway.

A girl came in wearing a short dress and heels. There were plenty of empty stools, but she sat down beside me. She was young and pretty in a ravaged way. We talked. She was a hooker, but at the moment I didn't care. She stated a price, I accepted, and we went to my room where I flopped onto the bed and commenced sipping bourbon from a bottle, and she stepped into the bathroom and shut the door. Sometime later she emerged naked and dropped her clothes on the floor. Then she lay down beside me, giving me a vapid smile. Her eyes were glassy and unfocused. "Let's fuck," she said. I paid her the fifteen bucks, and we did, or I suppose we did.

I don't remember anything afterward and must have passed out, but sometime in the night someone stirred beside me, and I remembered her. She had said her name was Glenda, that she was from a place I no longer remember. Hell, we're all from somewhere. Who cares? These were the sorts of thoughts floating around in my damaged mind.

Then I felt a prick on the underside of my forearm.

It came from her side of the bed, and suddenly I was transported to paradise. I saw God, and He saw me. Angels and cherubim flitted about like celestial bats against a wondrous panorama of stars hanging patiently in a blue, three-dimensional field. Nothing mattered. Pain and yearning had been banished from this special universe; guilt and failure were unknown. All was serene and silent, suffused with love and goodwill. I adored Glenda unconditionally and knew in a telepathic way that she felt likewise. We would be together always, true soulmates bathed in bliss for eternity. Our meeting had been inevitable; we were astral twins just now realizing our bonded destiny. Grungy reality had vanished. . .until it returned.

I woke up suddenly, feeling weird. She was sleeping beside me. "You bitch, you stuck heroin in me while I was helpless!"

Her eyelids fluttered, and she slurred, "Yeah, baby, but once you get in the groove we can get high together all the time. I love you."

I couldn't imagine why she wanted me in her meretricious world of alternating ecstasy and torment, especially to the point of wasting heroin on me that she ordinarily would have saved for herself. Perhaps in her delusional state she mistook me for a potential sugar daddy. Or maybe she simply wanted someone to fly with her to paradise this one time, then crash with her down into hell. Someone to ride shotgun. The promise of love would last until she needed a fix and I didn't have the money, then she would be on the street again hustling. In our need we inevitably would abandon one another. Junkie love is a zero-sum relationship, and I wanted no part of it, not now, not ever. Anyway, how had "love" come up at all? Our arrangement had been a business transaction.

I said, "You want me to get hooked, same as you, so we can be co-dependent? That won't happen." I dumped her onto the floor. "Get out," I said. "Put on your clothes and get out, and don't come back."

It was my day off. I was grateful for my ordinary shitty life replete with hangovers, hemorrhoids, and occasional outbreaks of athlete's foot courtesy of Army shower rooms. Big deal.

I suffered through the present hangover and in the evening went to the bar and told Ida and Junior what had happened. I asked them not to serve Glenda and to please eject her the next time she showed up to prowl for johns.

When I told Josie he was horrified. I said her name is Glenda, that I see her around the resort every so often. I said, "She's a free-lancer. No pimp."

"I know who she is. Holy shit! Hooking is bad enough, but I can't have hard drugs floating around the resort. Some of our guests actually are decent people, odd as that seems. If I see Glenda anywhere on the grounds I'll give her the bum's rush."

———————

Knowing Ida had been a student of comparative literature, I figured she could give me some advice about what to read. I enjoyed novels but could always use tips on picking them. The literature classes I took that year at junior college had been an inspiration.

Ida jumped at the opportunity to advise me, saying

she was always willing to help people interested in books and suggested we start by perusing the resort's collection left by guests. There was a large open alcove adjacent to the reception area furnished with comfortable wicker chairs. Lining two walls were floor-to-ceiling book-stuffed shelves. Unsurprisingly, many of the guests were highly educated and had eclectic tastes. Use of this unofficial library operated on the honor system. Books were available on loan to guests and staff and meant to be returned; however, you could keep a book provided you left a another in its place. And, of course, most of the books were donations that guests had brought to read on vacation intending to leave.

I looked at the titles, scanning them for the first time. "Looks like reading could be a full-time job," I said. "So, if I start just parttime, when does it end?"

"Never," Ida said.

"That's sad."

"No, that's exhilarating. You'll die ignorant, same as you were born. You'll have come full circle. That's as complete as you can ever be."

"How about this one?" I pulled Thomas Pynchon's *The Crying of Lot 49* from the shelf.

Ida glanced over. "I don't advise starting a reading program with Pynchon. His stuff is dense. Raymond Chandler is maybe our greatest writer of noir, and I see several of his novels here. They're wonderful, and pay attention to the writing itself, not just the narrative. Chandler set the style for the modern noir genre." She handed me *Farewell My Lovely*. It was terrific. Over the next several days I devoured the three titles by

Chandler available in the resort's library. Then it was on to Fitzgerald's *The Great Gatsby* and Hemmingway's *A Farewell to Arms*, *For Whom the Bell Tolls*, and *Death in the Afternoon*, all presented before my eyes like ripe, low-hanging fruit. And what a harvest! Waiting their turns patiently were Graham Greene's *The Quiet American* and *The End of the Affair*.

As Ida was looking over the titles, she said, "Whoa! Didn't expect to find this here. She pulled down Benjamin Spock's *On Parenting* and said, "I sometimes think of having a kid, but in this shitty world it's probably a bad idea. Procreation is overrated. Really, what's its purpose other than a weak lunge for immortality?"

"It's the only world we have," I said. "Take it or leave it."

"Or procrastinate until it's too late, which is what I seem to be doing. There's no way I'd go the conventional route. Can you picture me with a dude lying on top? Ha! It'd have to be artificial insemination and the consent of a suitable sperm donor."

"Paint me a picture of that donor. Your offspring would have half his genes, so you'd need to be choosy."

She gazed over my head as if appraising something in the distance. "I don't know, maybe a grunge rocker or a lumberjack. Unkempt and manly, but smart and intriguing. Definitely not a junkie or alkie. But no up close getting touchy-feely to get the deed done. Test tube only."

"Who would babysit while you tend bar?"

She laughed, "You, of course, and you could read to the kid."

Sometime after starting my reading program I

mentioned to Ida that I was encountering words I didn't know. She said to buy a dictionary of modern American English and keep it handy. Make it a paperback for portability. She also advised going to a stationery store and buying two notebooks, one for jotting down ideas derived from my reading, the other to start a personal dictionary. I was to look up unknown words as I encountered them and record their definitions. She guaranteed that by writing them down my vocabulary would increase rapidly, and it was true.

During quieter happy hours Ida lectured me on literary theory, how a written story is a contract between author and reader. The author's imagination is manifested in the text, but it's up to the reader to envision the characters and scenes and interpret the narrative. The author's vision and interpretation are inevitably different from those of the readers. Everyone is unique. We see the world within the context of our own experiences, but that doesn't matter when picturing how a narrative plays out and the characters look and sound. The contract remains intact because it's the way all elements of narrative and characterization come together in the reader's mind that make a story. "Think about this," she said. "You read a novel in which a female character is blonde. If that's the only description the author presents, anything else about her must be imagined. However, you go to a movie and everything is obvious. If the lead actress is blonde then she's a blonde to everyone there, and all her other features and attributes are obvious too.

"I'll be specific. Suppose you picked up Ian Fleming's

novel *Casino Royale* in 1953, the year it was published and before the Bond films became a craze. You'd have had no image of Bond's personal appearance other than the paltry clues Fleming provides and what you imagined from putting them together. Fleming, of course, had a mental picture of his own creation, but readers had theirs, inevitably different from Fleming's and each other's. Then the first Bond movie came out. That was *Dr. No*, and imagination became superfluous. The world now knew what James Bond looks like. He looks exactly like Sean Connery. In other words, imagination isn't necessary when the actors and scenery appear identical to everyone. Reading requires extra mental expenditure. *It takes imagination!* That's why the reader participates actively in a written narrative but only passively when the narrative is embedded in an audiovisual medium such as film. Pick up a novel and you immediately begin fulfilling your part of the contract with the author." She slapped her hand on the bar for emphasis. "You can be semi-conscious and get the gist of a movie. No viewer contribution is required because the creative part has been done and presented to you on a platter. I'm spitballing here, but the German novelist Günther Grass has said that movies are a substitute for the imagination."

Chapter 8

———•◆•———

EASTERTIME HAD COME. SPRING Break was in full swing. The resort was filled to overflowing, and the staff shifted into riot control mode. It was the first full day of my friends' Florida vacation. Angel had looked me up on arrival and said he and Giovanni were going to a thrift shop to buy resort attire. Willie and Lenny had been at the bar since after lunch. I knocked off work around five, showered, and joined them for happy hour. Willie scooted over a stool gave me his seat, putting me between them.

He said, "Me and Lenny was just discussing traveling. We been around, the two of us, unlike Angel and Giovanni, who basically ain't been nowhere. Us two and a couple of other wiseguys from the neighborhood and my brother Larry, we once fly to Vegas for a three-day weekend. We leave Frankie to mind the booth in the parking lot. Frankie is usually off weekends and kicks back, but Larry, he needs a break. I'm the oldest brother, Larry's the baby, and Frankie, he's in between, so I pull extra weight when there's conflict, which I'm about to tell youse about. That trip, youse see, it comes wit a story. Lenny, of course, he knows it already 'cause he was there.

"The story goes like this. We no sooner arrive in Vegas that Thursday afternoon and check into our hotel than the phone is ringing, and it's Frankie all nervous. Larry gets on the line. 'What's the problem?' he says. Frankie says he's worried, what if he's robbed or something. Larry tells him that's why we furnish the booth wit that .38 under the cash drawer and the baseball bat in the corner. Frankie says, 'I'm an accountant. We're peaceful people, accountants. I ain't never shot nobody, and the only thing I ever hit wit a baseball bat is a baseball.' Larry tells him to relax, youse only gotta wound the perpetrator when youse shoots him, youse don't need to kill the bastid, and if swinging the bat, a guy's head is lots bigger and slower than a Ryne Duren fastball. You ain't likely to strike out.

"We're antsy to visit the casinos, but still no dice, so to speak, not wit Frankie whining long-distance through the phone wires. Says I to Larry, 'Gimme the receiver, and I say into it, look, Frankie, call Catalano's from the phone there in the booth and ast one of the wiseguys taking up space at the bar to come sit witchuse, maybe bring youse dinner. Him and youse can eat take-away and share a bottle of chianti. Offer to pay for the spread and slip him fifty clams.' Then Frankie says, '*Fifty bucks*? You can't be serious! Minimum wage is a buck-fifteen, for chrissakes!' I tell him to relax and pay up, that the wiseguy, whoever he might be, is a specialist, not some schmuck or wino we hire to pick up trash in the lot. Finally, all is good. Frankie relaxes a little. We unpack, go down to the lobby to meet up wit the guys, and attack the tables. And guess who's the crooner on stage that night? Old Blue Eyes hisself."

He waved to Ida and Junior and raised his empty glass. "So, this traveling crew is a little different, and it involves another story. As I said, me and Lenny has flew before. Angel says he flies once, from Puerto Rico to New York, but he's just a baby and don't recall the experience. That leaves Giovanni, who come to America as a little kid by boat. You know, the old story of the Statue of Liberty and the American Dream and everybody aboard has hankies out sniffling and wiping their eyes wit gratitude. Same as my parents done on the boat from Sicily. This behavior applies most especially to the wops. The Irish, not so much. The Irish ain't known to be weepers. Did youse know that the Irish didn't learn to walk on their hindlegs till the wheelbarrow is invented? Ha! It's a joke, get it?

"Anyhow, Giovanni I thought was gonna shit his pants when our plane lifts off. He prays the whole way to Miami loud in Italian, moaning like a dying cow and squeezing his beads: *"Padre, ti prego, veglia su di me. So di aver peccato ma prometto di farmi perdonare, lo giuro!"* After a while it's driving us and everybody else nuts. Luckily, the cabin crew is serving Miami Sunrises to calm the natives, which is orange juice mixed wit champagne. Sounds disgusting, but ain't too bad after the first few."

"I didn't catch that prayer," I said.

"Oh sorry. Basically, watch over me God. I know I'm a sinner but promise to do better, meaning please save the body part planted here in the seat, namely, my ass. I ain't too worried about my soul at the moment, which I already told youse needs work.

"We rent the car in Miami and head for Key West, and Giovanni now thinks the Overseas Highway is gonna collapse and we'll die. Angel is very helpful. He points out some twisted train tracks we pass and says, 'Hercules, see them tracks? There usta be a train to Key West, but a hurricane come through and that's all it left behind.' That sets off another round of prayers accompanied by howling and weeping, which Angel enjoys lots more than me and Lenny."

––––––––––

The next day I had responsibilities and didn't see the guys until late when I finally mopped the last flooded bathroom and cleared the drain. The guys, as I said, had checked in two days previously, and although I'd passed a little time with Willie and Lenny I'd barely been in contact with Angel except to receive a man hug and a 'great to see youse' and the announcement he was going shopping.

I found him in the bar at happy hour sipping a beer and chatting with Ida. He was dressed for hot weather in thrift shop sandals, shorts, and t-shirt. I sat down beside him, and Ida brought me a cold draft. I said to Angel, "I heard about your trip down, that it was a little stressful."

He turned to me. "Youse heard it from Willie White Eyes, right? Who else? Why do I even ast."

Ida said, "Mind if I listen in? It's slow at the moment, and I need some entertainment."

Angel said, "Naw, sweetheart. It's okay."

Ida blew up. *"Sweetheart?"* she yelled, and slammed her fist down on the bar top. "I'm not your fucking sweetheart! I have thirty pounds on your scrawny ass and could take you down in a second!"

Angel turned to me and spread his arms. "What the fuck did I say?"

Ida interrupted. "You offended me, you prick. I'm a dyke and nobody's sweetheart."

Angel turned to her. "I'm really sorry, ma'am."

"Ma'am? *Ma'am*, for chrissakes? You're digging the hole deeper." She slapped herself in the forehead. "Ah, hell, the damn cramps are making me touchy today. My period is coming on. No harm, no foul. Shake?" She held out her hand.

"Jesus, youse got a helluva grip, Ida. I'm inna fight I want youse on my side." We all laughed.

"So, about the trip," I said.

Angel stood. "Back in *un momento*. Gotta water my *caballo*.

When he was out of audio range Ida said, "I like your friends from New York. That story Willie told yesterday about going to Las Vegas and then the trip down here was a scream. I couldn't help but eavesdrop. As a connoisseur of language I appreciate regional accents. In college I took a course in the linguistics department taught by an eccentric little prof named Doctor Schwartz. The class was titled *American Dialects: Then and Now, Here and There*. He'd traveled around the country with a tape recorder asking people to speak into the mike. Later, he teased out the origins of the regional accents and word usage he'd encountered and put together these lectures. They were fascinating. When your mountain twang bounces off New York street-speak I hear poetry.

"Your accent is derived largely from the Scots-Irish who immigrated to the Appalachians during the eighteenth and nineteenth centuries. Like dropping the 'g' in gerunds, making 'carrying' into 'carryin' and omitting the 'y' in 'everything,' making it 'ever'thin.' The New York accent comes mostly from nineteenth-century London, although 'youse' originated with the Irish when they switched from speaking Gaelic to English. Gaelic has a plural for 'you' and so they added an 's' to its English equivalent. In college I read Sean O'Casey's plays, which center on the working class Irish in the early twentieth century, and 'yous,' as he spells it without the 'e,' is common in his characters' speech. It's street-Dublin Irish all the way."

"That's cool," I said. "I hadn't known any of this."

Ida said, "Yeah, all good stuff. Incidentally, what do Willie and Lenny do for a living?"

"You probably shouldn't ask."

"I thought so. I knew you and Angel worked together in a kitchen, but the little Italian guy, what about him? He seems out of place around the other three."

"Giovanni's a fit, in his own way. He's head waiter at Catalano's, the restaurant in Coney Island where I washed dishes and Angel still does. And Willie and Lenny are regular barflies there. Angel calls him Hercules, so you'll be hearing both names."

"He's somewhat out of his element, isn't he?"

"He'll get used to it."

Angel returned and sat down. "Yeah. So, the trip.

Festivities start when the plane takes off. Picture the layout. We're sitting in steerage, right? There's rows of two seats and a aisle in between, right? Hercules is sitting by a window, I'm on the aisle. I give him the better seat 'cause I figure he'll get a kick out of looking at the ground way down there. Instead, it totally wigs him out. He becomes convinced he's somehow gonna fall outta the plane and starts moaning and praying and squeezing his beads. Now, Willie is sitting in a aisle seat directly behind me, and Lenny has the window beside him. Youse wit me, Ida?"

"All the way, sweetheart." She was leaning on the bar, chin in hand, and grinning impishly. "I'm loving this shit."

Angel grinned back. "Okay. . .the story. Hercules, he won't quit his act, and in fact the volume of his moaning and praying in wop is getting louder. It's annoying the other inmates. The guy across the aisle from me looks like one of them hippies. He pokes me in the arm to get my attention, then says, 'Is he a spirit? Does he think the end is near? Maybe I should be praying too, if that's what he's doing. I mean, he looks like he's got it together.' The guy is obviously stoned, and I'm thinking, how do I become stuck between two tootie-fruities? Lucky me, I tell myself. The guy pokes me again. 'I figured it out,' he says. 'He's a priest, right?'

"I glance over at Hercules robed in that moth-eaten tux and think, I suppose if someone's high enough he might mistake Hercules for a man of the cloth, although truthfully his outfit is more holes than cloth. 'He's a waiter,' I tell the guy, 'and this is his first airplane ride. He's nervous, that's all. I'm Catholic and know this: God handed us two ways of keeping our shit together. There's prayer, and there's alcohol. For youse I recommend the second choice considering that my friend here seems to have the first one covered.'

"The guy immediately pushes the button that summons a stewardess. When she arrives, he says, 'Nurse, a double bourbon on the rocks, please, and bring refills each time youse seen I went dry.'

"About then Willie sticks his face between the seats and whispers, 'Shut the fuck up, Giovanni.' I said Willie 'whispers' it, but when Willie whispers it's like a normal person shouting as loud as possible. A stewardess immediately approaches Willie and actually does whisper. She says, 'Is there a problem, sir?' And Willie 'whispers' back, nearly breaking her eardrum, 'Naw, it's just my compadre being a numb-nuts,' and a hunnert passengers, probably all of them New Yorkers, cracks up."

Changing the subject, I said, "I see Giovanni's now walking around in sandals, shorts, and a loud Hawaiian shirt. How did y'all manage to strip that moldy tux off him?"

"It was surprisingly easy," Angel said. "When we get to the resort I discover I ain't dressed proper and need some spring fashions, so I come to the bar and ast Ida's sidekick Junior where's a thrift shop. He knows one wit a big selection. I get the address and suggest to Hercules that me and him go shopping, him still in his tux, of course. We hail a cab.

"During the ride I'm telling Hercules how he needs to become part of the program, he's on vacation and has to let down his hair a little. This confuses him, probably 'cause he's totally bald and still don't understand English all that good. Well, I explain, such advice about letting down the hair would apply to a person in actual fact supposing he has hair, which in his situation, I remind him, he don't, and that otherwise it's a expression meaning have a good time, and to achieve this, I go on to say, he needs to suck it up, chill out, and ponder about what maybe having hair might be like, even though the possibility for him raises an impossible situation. 'Capisce?' I say, using one of his own words."

On hearing this Ida collapsed into hysterics. "You're killing me, Angel. I wish I had a tape recorder."

Angel ignored her. "As youse just heard, I go out of my way to make this crystal clear so there's no misunderstanding." At this, Ida has to walk away to catch her breath. Angel continues as if nothing happened. "All this time Hercules is in America he still blunders around confused like a barnyard fowl. Lotta times shit flies right over his hairless skull as if he's still back in where-the-fuck-am-I Sicily. However, this time he must have received the message 'cause he don't say even a peep during the rest of the cab ride and picks out some duds right away when we get there to the store. Youse seen him strutting around already on his chicken legs and scruffy sandals. Now he blends right in wit the rest of the weirdos and maybe oughta migrate here permanent, except that Coney Island is just as weird as Key West, so he might as well stay there." Angel slid off the stool. "Later. Please run me a tab, Ida. I gotta go shower and, as the saying goes, prepare to display some sartorial splendor. Can't let Hercules dazzle the *chicas* in his new getup and leave poor me horny and sobbing on the sidelines."

"Get the hell out of here, Angel," Ida said. "My sides can't take any additional pain."

Indeed, Giovanni had shed his tattered tux like a snake sheds its tired skin. The snake does it to provide new room for growth, but Giovanni's transformation had a reverse effect: the ecdysis made him seem smaller. The world now saw his skeletal arms and legs for the first time protruding like sticks from his too-large shorts and shirt. He looked like a scarecrow on vacation. Outsized feet clad in worn sandals and bald head wobbling atop a neck resembling a mail-box post added another garish dimension. The overall impression was bizarre, although in Key West, as Angel noted, not out of place.

Willie, Lenny, and I were at the bar when Angel plopped onto a stool beside us and exhaled loudly. "Whatsa matter?" said Willie. "You look bushed. The heat?" He looked Angel up and down. "Hey, nice threads."

"Thanks. I'm bushed alright. Delayed reaction. Clothes shopping wit Hercules is a marathon. I leave the bar this afternoon and go back to the room intent on a shower and a nap, and he starts complaining again. From what I can make out, maybe his new outfit ain't color-coordinated or something. I'll tell youse the whole story." He waved Ida over and ordered a drink. She delivered it then stuck around to listen. Angel raised the glass to her in thanks.

"As I said before to Ida and my ridge-running former roommate here, me and Hercules go in a cab to the thrift shop to get outfitted. He picks out a pair of shorts several sizes too big. I mean, they might be loose on Willie here. I mention this, but he ignores me. They're chartreuse and hang on him like bloomers. Next, a Hawaiian shirt that's pink, for chrissakes, wit purple polka dots and some orange palm trees. It's huge. He's ready to leave. I don't say nuttin this time, except he's gotta try the stuff on and look at hisself in the mirror. I'm hoping then he'll see the light, know what I mean? He replies that he don't need to, all is *copacetic*, but I drag his ass to the back of the store anyway.

"There's only one dressing room available. I go in wit him. When he drops trou I see that his formerly tighty whities ain't tight no more 'cause the elastic has rotted away, and they ain't white neither, they're gray and mostly holes. 'How long youse had these?' I say. He starts waving his arms and yelling, 'I don'ta remember! maybe twenty year!' I yell back, 'They're disgusting! Youse owns how many pairs of skivvies?' 'What is skivvies?' he says. 'Underwear,' I says. He tells me he has two.

"Turns out that back home he does his laundry in the bathroom sink, so the other pair he leaves in his room in Coney Island hanging over the shower rod to dry. He's planning to wear the skivvies he has on the whole two weeks we're in Florida. I tell him, toss them things in the trash can over in the corner while I fetch youse two new pairs still in the packages. He whines and bitches and has to ast what's wrong wit these ones. He cries poverty. I say, 'Okay, okay, I'll carry the weight for the new ones. The treat is on me.' I return and hand him the replacements and tell him, 'Meet youse outside the dressing room. Put one pair on now and change at the end of the week.'

"When he comes out he's wearing his tux. I ast if he tries on the shorts and shirt. He shakes his head. I say, 'Okay, I can see youse is carrying the shorts and shirt, but where's the other skivvies?' He tells me he's wearing both pairs so he don't forget where he stashes the spare. In other words, he goes to the inconvenience of getting naked to put on two pairs of skivvies but don't bother to try on the shorts and shirt while in that innocent state." Angel shook his head and ignores Ida, who's doubled over. "Unbelievable. But somebody's gotta look out for him. He's sorta like an *abuelo* to me, the ditzy old fart."

Angel turned on his stool and looked over the clientele. "Youse gotta admit that the birdbrains and fruitcakes down here, they're a different weird from Coney Island. Friendlier, right? In fact, it's a Coney Island witout the boardwalk. Everything is above board, so to speak. You can see it all witout getting sand in the shoes down among the pilings and pervs. And it ain't as dangerous neither. Take the manager of this this clown show, whatsisname, Josie. When we check in he rushes up to me and says, 'Youse must be Angel! I'm just so goddamn thrilled to meet youse!' Then he steps back all dramatic and turns sideways, throwing me the sheep-eye behind them Coke-bottle glasses and waggling his eyebrows. Finally, he extends his hand real slow wit the wrist bent, like a princess or something. I didn't know, was I was supposed to shake the fucking thing or kiss it?"

"Where's Giovanni now?" I say.

"He's in the kitchen at Diner Shores coaching the polack chef on how to cook Italian. The chef's name is Jan. They become chums on discovering that both their names mean 'gift from God' in their home language. How they figure this out, who knows?" He started snapping his fingers and singing the old Nat King Cole tune "Someone's in the Kitchen with Dinah." Ida had left us to serve a customer but came back and joined in. We made a pretty good quintet, and Lenny proved to be a surprisingly talented baritone. All we knew was the first few stanzas, so the performance was over quickly.

Ida said, "Jan was already working here when I started, but legend says he was a chef aboard a big tourist boat out of Miami. He stepped ashore for a smoke break, liked what he saw, and jumped ship. Junior was working the bar then and probably knows Jan's history better than anyone. He tells people that Jan never even went back aboard for his clothes so he, Junior, took him to that thrift shop and outfitted him for the tropics. Jan's an okay guy, but he yells in a lot in words nobody understands."

"No sweat," Angel said. "Hercules, he does the same. It should be a treat to hear them two arguing."

———————

For the two weeks Giovanni was in Key West he and Jan circled each other warily. The exchange of presumed insults and threatening gestures never stopped.

Diner Shores became a war zone of outsized egos and international distrust, or so it seemed to everyone else. I told myself this assessment was entirely presumptive: they can't understand each other and no one else can understand either of them, so how can they actually argue? Any disagreements must be expressed in poses, voice inflection, and hand waving. Josie, Angel, and I happened to be standing by one day and witnessed an especially intense episode.

"What just happened?" Josie said. He looked at Angel for an explanation.

"Yeah, well, I work every day wit Hercules and sometimes understand what he's saying, Italian and Spanish being similar, know what I mean? Roughly translated, Hercules is ripping Jan a new one 'cause him, Hercules, cooks up a dago specialty and Jan waltzes over and sprinkles parsley on it. As a result, Hercules calls Jan a *cazzo stupido*, a dumb fuck. Everybody knows the correct spice for this dish is basil, Hercules shouts in his face. Then he adds for good measure that this establishment, meaning Diner Shores, is a *parodia*, a travesty, Jan's own dishes are *merda di maiale*, and that he, Jan, needs to couth up. What Jan shouts back in Polish? Youse need to ast a polack."

I said, "What was that term he called Jan's cooking? *Merda*, uh. . . ."

"*Merda di maiale*? It means 'pig shit.'"

"Goodness! Oh my, how wonderfully fucking wonderful!" Josie smiled as visions of dollar signs danced in his head.

These performances were immensely entertaining. Word of a live impromptu comedy act spread across the island. Diner Shores was packed at all hours, and the equivalent of another roomful of people stood outside waiting to get in. Josie stopped taking restaurant reservations because in such a maelstrom nothing could be predicted, much less guaranteed.

We emptied the storeroom of spare chairs and set them outside on the pavement. When people complained about the heat Josie added a dozen rental tables with umbrellas. The resort had no permit to expand the seating but Josie figured screw it, he'll pay the fine and still come out ahead. He extended the restaurant's business hours. Additional wait staff was hired to handle the crush and put under Giovanni's supervision. Predictably, confusion and incompetence escalated. Jan screamed at Giovanni, who screamed back then screamed at the servers. They returned his insults, often in Spanish or Haitian French, not understanding what Giovanni had said but from the tone knowing it was demeaning. Diner Shores became a United Nations without translators.

The atmosphere was cacophonous. Getting Lenny to his table required two guys to assist, one on each side. Had he lost his balance and gotten into one of those windmills he would have flatted everyone and everything within reach. Orders were scrambled or forgotten. Food and drink were spilled or dripped randomly onto the seated diners without apology; overturned trays of dirty dishes rained on their heads. And their response to this abuse? They laughed and overtipped. My Brooklyn friends were astonished. Such behavior in Coney Island would have incited instantaneous retaliation, but violent reactions were not the Key West way. Willie took a peek at the free-for-all from a safe distance and arranged through Josie to get lunch delivered lunch to his room, and to have Junior drop off appropriate choices of wines to accompany it.

Nothing made sense, but Josie didn't care. He counted the receipts and basked in heavenly greed, the prospect of a pay raise from ownership dancing in his head. Never one to miss a marketing opportunity, he blanketed Key West with a flyer that read:

ATTENTION ALL CONCHS!

Appearing in person at Diner Shores through April 25th, the incomparable Giovanni, Headwaiter and Consulting Chef of renowned Catalano's Ristorante in Coney Island, New York, a culinary mecca for discerning diners since 1907. Some of Giovanni's favorite Sicilian dishes will be served as daily specials starting at noon, alongside resident chef Jan's unique creations from his home country of Poland. Come dine with Giovanni and Jan. Don't miss this experience!

Ocean Shores Resort
510 South Street
Key West
Phone (305) 493-3333

After the flyer hit the streets still more people poured in. The office phone rang continuously, and Josie hired an acquaintance to answer it and take messages so he could finally get to his paperwork. Like Josie, the guy addressed everyone as "sweetie" regardless of age or gender, and he shamelessly plugged the resort and its clothes-optional bar as the highlight of Key West, forget the monument marking the southernmost point in the U.S., forget the Key West Aquarium and Hemingway's house and its cadre of six-toed cats.

It's a day off for me, just another vacation day for Willie and Lenny. We're sitting naked at the bar. Lenny has become a local celebrity; rather, his ten-inch snausage has. It's even gained a moniker: Lenny's Famous because its length easily matches anything slathered in mustard offered by Nathan's Famous on the boardwalk back in Coney Island.

Lenny's barstool is turned to face the room, and this astonishing appendage lies draped over the edge of the seat like an earthworm on steroids or the proboscis of a dozing baby elephant. Both men and women cast admiring looks from afar and sometimes close up. One guy approaches and asks if he can touch it. "If youse want all youse fingers broke," Lenny tells him.

"Life is so unfair," Willie says in a false whine. "My feet don't even reach the rung of the stool, and I can't see my kielbasa 'cause my stomach is in the way. Lenny gets all the love and admiration."

"Yeah, but he takes the pressure off the rest of us", I said.

"I didn't think of that," said Willie. "Youse could be right." He slid off his stool and signaled Junior to keep his tab open. "Gotta get my beauty rest. Me and Lenny, we got a coupla hot dates tonight."

"Who are the lucky ladies?" I said.

"We don't know yet," Willie said. "The hookers don't show up till happy hour. That's when we make their acquaintance and negotiate the, uh, cost of the date."

Chapter 9

———◆◆———

MY FRIENDS HAD LONG since departed. It was a hot day in August, slack season now, and I'd been repainting some of the vacant rooms. I even returned at night sometimes, trying to keep up. Josie was being cheap again. He had let me hire an assistant the previous December, and now wanted to lay him off using as a reason that it was slack season. However, I reminded him, slack season is when most of the maintenance can be done. I had a list of tasks that required completion before the tourists season ticked up, and painting the scruffiest rooms was just one item. Many of the bathroom faucets needed new washers; dozens of drains were waiting to be snaked to prevent future backups. My new assistant and I were in process of replacing all the old wall outlets with grounded receptacles. There were broken window locks, which was a big deal because the entire resort was one storey, and guests risked burglary and worse from simple entry through windows. There were sticking doors, broken door locks, table and floor lamps needing rewiring. . . .The load seemed overwhelming, probably because it was.

I'd knocked off and finished showering and shaving when the phone rang, interrupting my musing about how things might be going at Catalano's and around the old neighborhood.

"It's Angel," the voice said. "We had a little excitement lately, and I thought to call and fill youse in."

I said, "Glad you did. I was just thinking of y'all up there when the phone rang."

"Yeah, well, I'm here guarding the bar, which is empty at the moment. Renato went to take a smoke and unload some stock, so I got a few minutes by myself. Anyhow, Willie and Lenny, our Terrible Twosome and poster children for the dumb and the lame, they knocked over an illicit gambling joint on Flatbush Avenue a while back.

"They'd gambled there previously to case out the operation, like, eye the security, locate escape routes, and such. Then the night of the holdup when they're ready to make their move Lenny whispers to Willie could they postpone the moment an hour or two 'cause he's ahead a coupla hunnert at the craps tables. Willie tells me he whispers back, 'Youse stupid shit, we're gonna take *all* the loot in just a minute, *capisce?*' and smacks Lenny on the back of his noggin for being a numbnuts. If it's not for all the background noise the whole block woulda been alerted to the impending heist. Youse remember Willie when he 'whispers.' So, at the appointed time they pull their irons and shout that the fun is over, will everybody please form a line and empty cash and valuables into this here gunny sack Willie is holding.

"The stickup takes only a few minutes. It's planned to be a timed operation. Willie looks at his watch, nods to Lenny, and the two of them scram out the back door into the alley, where waiting for them is. . .a dumpster. The getaway car is supposed to be there wit the engine running, only the driver gets the wrong address and turns up a no-show. Obviously, the aggrieved patrons get a close look at the perpetrators, seeing a short porky guy and a gangly gimp in dark suits, neither wearing a mask. However, they can't hardly file a complaint wit the law saying they was robbed while tossing illegal dice.

"A few minutes later the getaway driver arrives and double-parks, but our heroes has flew the coop, having made their escape on foot. Two lads in blue in a patrol car pull up to the dumpster. The cop riding shotgun gets out and the mook is told to roll down the window. He immediately throws his hands in the air and blurts out that he had nuttin to do wit it, he's just the wheel guy. 'Do wit what?' says the cop, confused. 'The stickup inside,' the driver says. 'Youse is double-parked, hold tight for the ticket,' our specimen of New York's finest tells him.

"Now, it's common knowledge that nobody gets ticketed for this offense. New Yorkers have a God-given right to double-park, I mean, it's practically in the state constitution, except the cop wit the ticket pad is a rookie and don't know any better. He's out for his quota, right? Meantime, his partner is sitting in the squad car drinking coffee and munching donuts and listening to the Yankees game on the radio. The rookie clues in his partner about a possible robbery. An alert is sent out, and Willie and Lenny get nabbed half a block away toting the swag. They're pounding along fast as they can, but neither was ever a track star. Lenny is hoofing on one leg and dragging the other. Willie, who's north of two-eighty, is sweating and thinking he's having a coronary. In fact, after this fiasco gets sorted out Willie goes on a diet and tells Hercules to never again serve him anything with alfredo sauce on pain of having his kneecaps busted. It lasts a day, Willie's diet, and the restaurant staff breathes a sigh of relief.

"But back to the main event. The perps is cuffed, booked, and tossed together into a grimy cell at Rikers Island. It's a slam-dunk case, right? They been caught wit the goodies in hand, know what I'm saying? They been identified by the doorman at the illegal club who has a record and cooperates. The driver of the getaway car, wishing to save his ass, fingers them too. They're toast. Except that no one comes forward to say they was robbed, and nobody wants to claim ownership of the gambling operation. So, the charges is reduced to possession of illegal firearms. The swag, I presume, goes into the city's coffers, and Willie and Lenny, as repeat offenders, they get sentenced to three months at Rikers."

I said, "Are they safe at Rikers? The place is a hell-hole."

Angel said, "They been sprung already, but youse is shitting me, right? We're talking here two Mafia guys, and made guys at that. Their reputations, as the saying goes, preceded them, and they owned the place. Rikers is like old home week to them. Lenny tells me later he thinks he's been in that same cell once before, maybe twice, 'cause the graffiti looks the same, although he can't be sure. Lenny admits to not being a big reader, and when it comes to art appreciation, forget it. Anyhow, nobody dared to fuck wit them. When I pay a visit the resident hoodlums and guards address them as 'mister' and 'sir' and offer to light their cigars.

"From the opening minute in stir our heroes live large. No hard benches for these jailbirds. They demand and receive two stuffed armchairs wit footstools. And no prison swill. Breakfast and lunch, they're delivered from a local diner. For the evening meal they're again given use of a phone, this time so they can call Catalano's and order take-away off the full menu. When everything is prepared and assembled the restaurant's owners whistle up their limo and send two waiters to Rikers where they enter the cell and set up a folding table wit linen tablecloth, two chairs, and a candle. The waiters is then led to the kitchen so's they can heat up the food.

"Dinner is preceded by apéritifs and Caesar salads, Lenny's wit his usual double anchovies. The main course is accompanied by fresh bread still warm from the oven and a decent red table wine. The dessert *du jour* follows, paired wit a chilled dessert wine like a Muscadelle or Spätlese Riesling. They top off the evening by kicking back wit five-dollar cigars and forty-year-old brandy served in crystal snifters.

"These guys have their own prison routine, see. Each morning a guard delivers two newspapers. The

New York Daily News they page through to see if any
of their friends is mentioned in the police report, then
read Jimmy Breslin's column for a chuckle. Afterward,
fortified by cigars and more coffee and bagels, they
study the *Daily Racing Form*. Homework finished, they
signal the guard, who opens the cell door, and they
follow him to a bunch of little private cubicles wit
phones in them, not the open wall phones they use
to order chow. There they enjoy some private time
talking to their bookies and laying bets.

"By then it's lunchtime. The diner that delivers
makes a killer pastrami sandwich, which goes down
smooth wit a chilled pinot grigio kept at temperature
in a ice bucket left for them by Catalano's waiters and
refilled wit fresh cubes by the guards. A few hands of
cards wit their captors and its naptime. That's how life
goes in the slammer if youse got connections.

"Anyhow, they was hardly even there. The *capo*
running Coney Island is mildly annoyed that they
free-lance and get caught. However, they're still his
wiseguys, so he sics one of his shyster lawyers on
the prosecutor. Sabers rattle, stacks of Benjamins
change hands, and the sentences get squeezed down
to a month.

"Turns out the operation they knock over is being
run by some Irish low-lifes, so no toes of another
Mafia family was stepped on. It's a wonder the wops
controlling that neighborhood hadn't took it down
sooner. When he sings at interrogation, the doorman
mentions that the mugs in charge of the joint don't
appreciate Willie politely telling their patrons to
think of what's happening as sort of like Mass and

his sack as a collection plate. 'Cash and jewelry much appreciated by the parish,' he supposedly announces. Meantime, as Willie is stuffing the collection plate, so to speak, Lenny sits on a crap table resting his foot and keeping the drop on everyone. According to the doorman, after every penitent has contributed in cash and hard-goods, Willie looks around and says, 'Attention, ladies: the parish also accepts ermines and minks.' When nabbed, Willie is toting the sack and also laboring under the weight of half a dozen fur coats. Them things is heavy. Lenny, he's just trying to stay upright."

Chapter 10

THE REST OF SUMMER faded into autumn, and autumn became winter. Angel phoned Josie and reserved two weeks in April for a second year, and to let him know that he and the guys had enjoyed that first stay so much they were thinking of making a vacation in Key West—or Paradise South, as Willie had christened it—an annual event.

When spring eventually came around, the Florida Keys shrugged. For someone like me imprinted on southern Appalachian hardwood forests and four distinct seasons, the realization that the Keys essentially have just one season became disheartening. It being May, I missed the rhododendrons and dogwoods and the many perennials. To see spring flowers in Key West requires visiting a florist. Springtime in New York is notable too, although it pales when compared to the mountains.

I was thinking more often about Julie and Amy and how I missed them, beating myself up for being such an idiot and running off. I ached to take them to those shadowed niches in the Appalachians as winter gives way suddenly and show them columbine and trillium in the understorey, to walk through the towns and villages holding hands admiring the yards bursting with jonquils, tulips, and daffodils. Then, as summer advances, pausing to take in the irises in their many varieties, with the lilies to follow. I could envision their blue eyes widening, almost hear the little exhalations of pleasure.

It occurred to me that perhaps I was reading too much, allowing daydreams to infiltrate the printed passages and render them into imagined experiences that will never happen. Surely, I hoped, moments must occur when time stops and dreams merge into reality. Then events must explode into palpable sensations of vision and hearing and their more subtle accoutrements of smell, touch, and taste.

The urge to go north was irresistible. Josie and I talked. He didn't want me to leave, now admitting that summer was the time to catch up on maintenance. I told him my decision was final, although I might come back in the fall. Meantime, he could contact my former helper, who was doing maintenance at another resort on the island. We had stayed in contact, and I knew he was looking for something else. I gave Josie his number.

Ida and Junior had scheduled vacations to visit family, Ida in Philly, Junior in Minneapolis. Same with the permanent kitchen help except Jan. Having nowhere else to go, he would be staying. The island's population was shrinking as summer approached. I was flush with more earnings than I'd ever had, so instead of thumbing back north I took the bus, although not before alerting Angel, who reported that the sheets on his spare bed at the hotel were reasonably clean, and that I would be welcomed back in the kitchen. I said fine, line me up a pair of those finger-to-elbow rubber gloves and notify Giovanni.

———————

Summer and autumn came and went, and I was still in Coney Island in a kind of stasis. It was my first winter back in the north. I can't recall which month, but I was flipping through memories of Key West. As I mentioned, I had left after that second tourist season, letting Josie and the staff know I'd probably be coming back for another go, but at that time the urge to see Coney Island and hang out with the crew at Catalano's was too strong. Now, inertia seemed to be keeping me there.

The night had been slow and the restaurant and bar finally emptied. Outside, snow was falling, and the sidewalks and street were quiet. Giovanni had sent the waiters and bussers home; the chefs had shut down their equipment, cleaned it, and departed, and Angel told Mario and Margarito to clock out, that he and I would finish up.

The bussers had left without clearing the last two tables, so Giovanni asked me to do it. They were near the back of the main dining area directly in front of three private alcoves. Each was separated from the rest of the dining area by a pair curtains behind which was a table and a small booth for two facing out. For the most part they were used by married wiseguys to rendezvous with their girlfriends. I thought the restaurant was empty except for a few lingering staff—specifically, Giovanni, Renato, Angel, and me—but the middle alcove was occupied. I could hear murmuring inside.

The curtains opened and closed in unison by pulling a string on a set of pulleys, identical to living room drapes. However, the halves of this pair didn't meet perfectly in the center, and between them was an open space of two inches or so. They also stopped a good three feet above the floor, as if a person's bottom half doesn't require privacy. Having been a kitchen denizen, I hadn't noticed any of this until accidentally dropping a napkin that night. When I bent down to pick it up I saw two exquisite stockinged legs ending in spike heels, one of which was draped over a pair of dark trousered legs ending in polished cordovans. When I stood and glanced through the open sliver between the curtains there was a blonde head pressed against a darker one. The lips of the blonde were nibbling at an ear attached to Father Joe; the legs and the lips undeniably were Doctor Susie's. I gathered the rest of the dishes as quietly as I could and crept away.

When I went back to the kitchen Angel was leaning over the sink scrubbing a pot. "You won't believe what I just saw," I said to his back. He grunted. When I said it was about Father Joe and Doctor Susie he did an about-face. His full attention now assured, I reprised the scene in detail.

Afterward, he looked down at the floor and shook his head. "Fucking unbelievable. You're absolutely sure it was them?" I nodded. He raised his head and looked at me, then crossed himself. "I'll be goddamn. Father Joe, that rascal, and right under our noses. My priestly cousin ain't gonna be happy hearing about it. Maybe I won't tell him. Yeah, that's probably better. Well, all I can say is, if God exists we now got undeniable proof he's Catholic and looking out for the good guys. Papa J and Doc Susie. Wow!"

The next night Angel peeled off his gloves and said, "Let's step outside for a smoke," nodding his head toward the door to the alley. "I need youse to meet somebody, a new arrival." He reached under the sink and took out a folded Army blanket I hadn't noticed. We crossed the alley to a dark area where a lump of remnant clothing was barely visible inside a large cardboard box tipped onto its side. "Hey, Greg, it's me, Angel. Remember me? I brung youse dinner last night. You awake?" The lump moved and metamorphosed into a human being. He was an unkempt white guy with stringy blond hair huddling inside an Army parka of Korean War vintage. "Look, I brung youse a blanket." The guy smiled and said thank you. He sounded gentle and educated. "This here is my pal from the restaurant." Angel introduced us, and we shook hands, Greg from his sitting position. "I'll get youse some food and wine a little later. Meantime, try to keep warm and have a smoke, okay?" He handed Greg a cigarette and lit it for him.

Greg inhaled and nodded. "Thanks, Angel. And don't worry, I'll police the area when my strength comes back some. Right now I got the shakes a little."

"No hurry, buddy. Whenever youse is up to it."

Angel explained his relationship with Greg after we returned to the kitchen. I'd stayed in the night before nursing a cold, and Angel had found him sleeping in the alley when stepping outside for a cigarette. Angel had a good heart. He didn't yet know Greg's story, how he came to live on the street, but he couldn't stand the thought of the guy scavenging scraps from garbage cans. He planned to deliver to Greg two meals a day, excess food the chefs would set aside that would be thrown out anyway at the end of the night. Renato would help too by saving leftover wine left in bottles returned by the bussers. Greg wouldn't care if they were mixed together and poured into a single bottle. As a wino he just anticipated the rush of the alcohol. Renato also would save partly full bottles rejected by the diners. He intended to keep all this under the bar for Angel to collect. In turn for the restaurant's kindness Greg had offered to police the area around the dumpster. Not that such a service was needed. New York's big streetsweepers came through often enough, but Greg felt guilty, like he was sponging, and wanted to contribute something.

Angel gave a helpless shrug. "I realize me and Renato ain't helping wit Greg's wine addiction, but I want him to be happy. What the fuck, we're a dishwasher and a bartender, not therapists."

———————

Angel's father had died the previous October. After a funeral ceremony in Bed-Stuy his mother flew with the body back to Puerto Rico where he was to be buried. She returned for a couple of unhappy months before packing her belongings and moving in with her sister's family in San Juan, breaking the lease in Brooklyn. Angel said he understood, that she was never comfortable in New York.

His local family was reduced to Angelina, now married with a baby. Her husband played guitar in a band at that club in Bed-Stuy where she had taken me on our date. In Angel's opinion the guy was a *pendejo*. In any case, Angelina's party-girl days were finished. She was stuck at home and no grandma around to babysit, allowing her to escape now and then. It was depressing, Angel said. Angelina knew her husband was screwing around with skanks from the club, hangers-on and pseudo-groupies. Angel hoped he didn't bring home a dose of the clap. In private he again said he wished I'd married her. I didn't tell him that under no circumstances would I have married his sister.

Sometime in late winter or early spring, maybe March, Angel said that for the first time he felt restless. Catalano's was changing. Some of the bar regulars, for different reasons, weren't coming around as often, or at all. Willie and Lennie were semi-retired and spending increasingly more time in Key West. He felt lonely without those guys around. Then Mario and Margarito disappeared. One day they simply didn't show up. We speculated about possible reasons. They found better jobs or got homesick and returned to Guatemala. More likely, INS picked them up and they were in detention or already deported. We settled on this last possibility because they hadn't at least stopped by to collect their recent paychecks.

Maybe, Angel said, he ought to come south too and work in Key West. Shit, he could wash dishes there as easily as in Coney Island and do it in a better climate. What did I think? I said it sounded okay, but he couldn't bunk with me because I lived in company housing, so to speak, and Josie wouldn't allow it, probably not even if he ended up employed at the resort in some capacity. Not unless the gig was a grade or so above hourly kitchen help. Angel said he understood.

I asked him, what happens to Greg if you split? He said Renato and the chefs would look after him, and we could take Greg to a thrift shop before leaving, buy him some warm winter clothes, another coat, and blankets. A sleeping bag might be warmer. And socks. Homeless people are always wanting socks. He said that at discount stores you can buy them new, the thick wool kind, six pairs to a bag. And Greg should have a warm watch cap too, and a scarf, and t-shirts to wear as a first layer, then maybe a flannel shirt, a heavy sweater, and finally the coat. Last but not least, better shoes. Maybe shoes and a pair of rubber boots too for wet weather.

As it turned out, Angel stayed where he was, mainly because I did too. It's because my life got turned upside-down.

———

Summer in Coney Island is exciting. We thought it would be our last for at least another year. On a Monday evening in mid-June Angel and I were loafing half a block east of Catalano's taking in the scene and sharing a pint of Jack in a brown bag. Darkness had fallen, and the sidewalks were jammed with tourists and Brooklynites enjoying the fine weather.

To stay clear of the foot traffic we had our backs flattened against a storefront window, but still with a view of the street. Surf Avenue itself was a slow-moving parking lot, every vehicle honking out the frustration of its driver over some annoyance or other. Jaywalking pedestrians did their part to disrupt traffic flow, schlepping among the cars oblivious to insults the drivers shouted at them. Elevated subway trains roared overhead, and police and ambulance sirens shifted the air pressure around. From Luna Park on the boardwalk came the distinctive sound of the Coney Island Cyclone, the famous roller coaster located next to the aquarium, a clatter of metal wheels mingled with the shrieks of its riders.

Then along came Father Joe, who famously surfed Surf Avenue in a 1959 Cadillac Eldorado Biaritz ragtop sporting tailfins that surely were the envy of every upwardly striving whale. The paint was lustrous midnight blue, the color of the deep sea, perhaps selected in tribute to his career as an ocean scientist. This elegant machine drifted silently on whitewalls shaded by fender skirts also of midnight blue. The interior was appointed in pristine leather the color of fresh cream, maybe symbolizing beach sand glowing under the summer sun. A pair of fuzzy dice representative of who knows what hung from the rearview mirror, shimmying to vibrations of ear-shattering rock emanating from the radio. And behind the wheel sat its owner in shirtsleeves and sporting shades, shoulders humping and head bobbing in rhythm to the beat.

Hoodlums and street hustlers and wiseguy wannabes stood on the corners whistling shrilly and shouting admiration as this private motorcade of one slid past. "Hey, Father Joe, how're they hanging?" "Hey there, good Father, I need to confess!" "Papa J, bless me so I get lucky tonight!"

He waved like a movie star to his throng and tooted the horn. Every parking space was taken for many blocks in both directions, but directly in front of Catalano's was a no parking zone marked by a fire hydrant and section of curb painted yellow. The Caddy slipped in as if shoehorned. Father Joe shut off the engine and stepped out leaving the top down and everything inside within easy reach.

"I love it!" said Angel. "Nobody but Papa J gets away wit this. The cops recognize his ride and won't ticket it. The bad guys know it too and don't dare steal nuttin or vandalize it, 'cause if Father Joe don't banish them to hell personally for dissing him, his shiftless homeboys standing around taking up space will pound the bejesus out of them. In fact, nobody touches this rolling Holy Grail while the good Father is inside Catalano's enjoying hisself. Guaranteed."

Angel was feeling it. "What a scene!" he said gleefully. "A reminder to us all that God lives in Brooklyn, probably at jet stream altitude above the pollution. We know this, how? 'Cause Father J arrives at the front door of Catalano's, parks his chariot illegally, then eats and drinks on the cuff into the wee hours. He's the prince of Coney Island, a good guy, sure, but why do the owners extend him this courtesy?

I'll remind youse of one reason why. He makes the shenanigans of the greaseball homies legit in a way only Catholics understand.

"Father Joe forgives their little escapades and makes wiseguy work seem like a day at the office. What's a bullet to the brain of some dirtbag in a deserted alley? A custom fitting of cement shoes? 'Scuse me, sir, but what size is youse feet? We offer washtubs in several models. Say what? We can't hear youse wit that canary taped inside youse mouth. No, sorry, we don't offer washtubs inna choice of colors. And by the way, we only use Portland cement. The stuff sets up underwater in case the mix ain't totally dry and we hafta make the dump ahead of schedule. Then there's the broken kneecaps when a guy accidentally trips over a three-foot length of pipe moving at mysterious velocity toward his legs. Why? Probably he's late wit the vigorish, and the *capo*, he don't like deadbeats. Hey, who notices? The wiseguys, they say, 'We didn't mean to offend God, and ain't nobody going to miss them rat-bastids anyways. It's just business, for chris-sakes, and we gotta earn a living.' As for old dishpan hands Angel, it's summer and I'm in love."

"Who's the lucky recipient?"

"Little Cuban girl I met in the drugstore around the corner from where my parents and Angelina usta live. She come by boat or raft or some damn thing to Florida, and now she's bunking wit relations in Bed-Stuy. Her Spanish is strange. I can't understand half of what she says."

"Is this love permanent? The real deal?"

"Permanent for now. Still thinking love is forever,

huh? Whatsa matter witchuse?" He gave me a remonstrative slap on the shoulder. "I thought I learned youse better. Must be a guilt hangup from running out on that broad and her kid when youse was up here last time. I sometimes think that hillbilly accent is phony and actually youse is a Irishman from Queens yearning to move in wit his mother and expunge the sin of impermanent relationships at daily Mass."

"That reminds me. What became of Maria and her son while I was in Florida?"

"Oh her. What youse might expect. When I don't step up and marry her and get a better job she goes back to bumble-fuck Puerto Rico to live wit her family, that place I told youse about where the citizens don't realize it when they die 'cause nuttin changes."

It was starting out a beautiful day in mid-July. The previous two weeks had been hot and sultry, the persistent heat like a savage fever. But a thunderstorm in the night had broken it, and the sky was now blue and cloudless. I was standing in front of Nathan's Famous looking at the menu on the wall behind the counter already knowing the choice would be two chili dogs with onions and spicy mustard. Suddenly, I was grabbed around the waist. I looked down to see a little girl clutching me, although not so little as the first incident. Then I glanced over and saw Julie standing beside me. I said, "I knew it couldn't be a dog leash this time, unless a Great Dane was on the end of it."

Julie laughed; Amy released me and stepped back. I gathered them into a single hug. "This is like a scene out of *Twilight Zone!* Here we are, meeting again in the same location."

Julie said, "Yep, it's another Monday bank holiday, and here we are. There's no place like the boardwalk at Coney Island on a summer day."

"Angel told me he'd heard you were married and living on Staten Island."

"I was, and we were, but that was a while ago. The marriage only lasted a year, and after the divorce Amy and I moved back to Brooklyn. We live in Sheepshead Bay now."

I offered to buy them lunch. We grabbed a table and began filling in the blanks of those missing years. I told them about Key West and life at Ocean Shores Resort. Julie said it sounded like a hoot and they'd love to see it sometime. Julie had risen to head teller at the bank where she worked. With her bachelor's degree in finance she hoped to eventually step into something bigger, such as loan officer, wealth management, or even head of a branch one day.

We sat talking until Amy became antsy, then ambled along the boardwalk. I felt like a sleepwalker trapped in a dream from a past that suddenly zooms at lightning speed into the present leaving too many unfilled spaces in between. I realized I'd wasted the intervening years stumbling around aimlessly, bumping against this experience and that but never straightening out the trajectory and moving linearly toward an objective. My life was no better organized and thoughtful than an animal's: eat, defecate, sleep, keep moving. . .repeat. From this moment forward I wanted dreams with relevance, dreams of substance so real I could try them on and stand around in them, share them, dreams that are goal-directed. What I suddenly wanted was to become conscious and responsible.

I looked at Julie. She was still slim and beautiful, maybe even prettier than I remembered. The beginnings of faint lines around her eyes and the few gray hairs seemed less like markers of age than of acquired wisdom and tolerance. I wanted desperately to pick her up and tell her how much I loved her, how much I'd missed her, and then grab up Amy and tell her the same. Something in the air was about to explode.

Amy said, "You still have that funny hillbilly accent. Ah reckon me'un Mom'll jist hafta git usta hit all over agin." She paused a moment. "You know, this really would sound better with a mouthful of marbles."

I said, "Ah kin tell thet ain't nobody done spanked that bottom enuf in them years we ain't saw one another. Ah kin fix that reeeel quick, iffen y'all keeps talkin back."

"Y'all hafta kitch me first, 'cause I got me a hankerin to run off yonder." And she did. She ran ahead up the boardwalk, looking back and laughing. I was laughing too, but Julie's sides were splitting.

We stopped so she could catch her breath. "I'm sorry, but I'm really not responsible. She turned out this way all on her own."

"She's perfect," I said. I looked at her. "And so are you."

Amy returned and grabbed my hand. She said, "You were a real shit for disappearing on us. We cried for days and days."

My heart sank to hear this. "An exceptionally smart person reminded me of that not long ago."

"You told somebody?"

"Once, and letting it out opened my eyes about what a terrible mistake I'd made."

"Why did you do it, run away like a scared rabbit?"

"I've spent the years since figuring that out. It's nothing you or your mom did wrong." I glanced at Julie, who had turned her head away and I couldn't see her face. "The blame's all on me. I was an only child growing up in a West Virginia coal camp. My home life had been miserable. I was afraid of becoming my parents. Mom was a drunk and a bully, Pa a weakling who didn't stand up to her. I feared always being an unreliable loser, and running out on y'all seemed like the final proof. It was too late by the time I realized things didn't have to have turned out this way."

"We thought you loved us."

"I did and always have. But you see, I couldn't face being responsible for someone else, namely you two. I'd never loved anyone before and was scared of not meeting expectations and failing. I was overwhelmed."

Amy squeezed my hand. "Afraid of a beautiful woman and a little kid who both loved you and wanted you to be there?"

"Afraid of disappointing you."

"Mom and I didn't expect anything special. Don't make it so hard. We only wanted you to love us back and be good to us and prove we could count on you. We just wanted to be a family, right Mom?" Julie was crying quietly and nodded.

"You could come back to us, couldn't he, Mom?" She bent forward and looked around me at Julie, who remained silent. "Mom? Well, you two figure it out," and she went skipping down the boardwalk.

I said, "She still makes me feel like I'm the inexperienced, irrational child and she's the wise, sensible adult."

Julie laughed through her tears. "I know that feeling. She's certainly put us on the spot." She dropped my hand and put her arm around my waist. I put mine around hers. "You were always the one," she said.

Amy returned and we continued our stroll. I had my ladies back, for the moment at least, holding their hands, one to each side. Amy looked up at me, shading her eyes with her other hand. "So, when are you moving in with us?" Julie smiled and shook her head at the audacity.

"Ah reckon when y'all was to give me a invite, not a tad afore." I'd said it to keep the conversation moving, not really expecting anything.

Amy said, "Well, think about this. I'll make it easy enough even for a hillbilly. We practically lived together once. I mean, you slept over, so you and Mom have already shacked up. You can skip the courtship and go straight to shacking up again. How much simpler could it get? Bring your stuff over and we'll pick up where we were before. *Except this time don't leave!* Got it?" She gave my hand a hard squeeze.

It took a long second to understand, then I said, "Yup, got it."

"Okay, now carry me the rest of the way like the first time and we might have a deal."

"In your dreams," I said.

I felt a tug on my other hand. Julie had stopped. She was now looking up at me and shading her eyes. "So, when y'all moving in with us? As of now consider you done been give the invite." She was smiling. How could she be so calm and gracious, so kind? How could this good fortune be happening so quickly? What had I done to deserve them after running out? I hoped Julie wouldn't wake up one day and discover she'd made a mistake by taking me back. Everything was now up to me to see that never happened.

"Give me your phone number and address," I said. "I need a few days to settle things at Catalano's."

"Good, we're over the threshold," Amy said. "This is progress. If you won't carry me at least buy Mom and me ice cream."

I called Julie the next afternoon around five just to talk. I remembered her mentioning that she got off work at three-thirty. She had just walked in from the grocery store when her phone rang. I was at work. The bar was empty except for Renato working his side of it and a wiseguy bellied up. Renato had said, sure, use the phone if it's a local call.

She started the conversation by commenting about how nice it had been yesterday and how excited she and Amy were about me coming back to them. I said I was just as excited and couldn't wait. Then she told me about her second husband. "It was awkward from the start. This time around I blame myself for thinking I needed a husband and Amy needed a father figure in her life. She did, but not just anyone. It's *you* she needed. And I didn't need just a husband, I needed *you*. I married on the rebound a couple of months after you disappeared. It was stupid, irrational, and strictly emotional and happened during a weak moment of feeling sorry for myself. A common refrain when single women with kids get together over glasses of wine is how common such scenes are. We inevitably ask ourselves, why are educated, supposedly intelligent women so blind when it comes to making life-changing decisions about men?" I assured her that this time I wouldn't let her down. It was a solemn promise, and I intended to keep it.

Chapter 11

———◆◆———

THE EFFECT OF MY moving in had been nerve-wracking, although we all joked and tried to blow the rough edges off as nothing serious. It was, of course. Deadly serious. We were about to reorder our lives as a functioning family and all that entailed: divvying up routine responsibilities, learning each other's habits and preferences and minor annoyances. . . .Everything that accompanies cohabitation. Inevitably, there were moments of misunderstanding. An example is once when Julie announced she was going grocery shopping and asked if I needed anything. Something wrenched inside, and I replied without thinking, "Please make sure there's always enough cereal and milk for Amy's breakfast."

She gave me a puzzled look. "That's a strange request. Of course. I always check those items. What prompted the question?" I said I'd explain to her later, which I did.

First and most important, I needed to find a job

and start contributing to the household expenses. The apartment Julie rented was the ground floor of a duplex, certainly big enough for three. There was a living room, an eat-in kitchen and pantry, two full bathrooms, and two bedrooms.

The first evening after my stuff had been hauled inside we went to a local restaurant for dinner. Julie and I were sitting on the couch afterward smoking and sipping glasses of wine when Amy's bedtime arrived. She bounced over and kissed Julie goodnight on the cheek. "I love you, Mom," she said. She then plopped onto my lap. "I love you too, goober man." She pushed my nose flat using an index finger and said, "But if you do us dirt again, you're roadkill."

"Okay, okay, I've got it. Sheesh, you sound like a wiseguy from Coney Island."

"Even worse. You can't ever imagine." She giggled and skipped off toward her room, turning when half-way there and shaking her finger at us. "I'll expect you both to tuck me in at night. It's your duty as parents, so no shirking."

"*Goober* man?" I said. "Where did that come from?"

"Beats me," said Julie.

A half-dozen daily newspapers were being published in the New York area during the 1960s. Since that day when I bumped into Julie and Amy again on the boardwalk I had been skimming the classifieds looking for something in auto mechanics. I got a bus schedule and map of Sheepshead Bay to start learning my way around. The Brooklyn neighborhood of Sheepshead

Bay is named after a local fish called the sheepshead, which inhabits the eponymous bay. The southern end of the neighborhood abuts the Manhattan Beach neighborhood of Coney Island, meaning it's the part of Brooklyn nearest where I had been living. From the closest subway stop from us to the one at Boardwalk and West 8th Street was a twenty-minute ride.

We had no immediate plans to buy a car. Amy took a school bus, and Julie and I would continue using city buses, an awkward situation for her when she needed to get groceries or otherwise run errands.

I saw an ad for a mechanic placed by a Chevy dealer nearby with good local bus service from a stop at the corner near us. I called and was asked to come for an interview. I went, taking my Army file along as proof of my training as a mechanic. I was given an application to fill out while waiting to meet the employment manager. In addition to my Army experience I mentioned on the application having taken auto mechanics in high school and working as a mechanic off and on during those years and during my year of college prior to the Army.

A guy from the coal camp in his early thirties had opened a gas station with a single-bay garage where he did light mechanical work. It was a sideline for his full-time job in the mines, but gave him a nice second income. When his shifts at the mine interfered with open hours at the gas station and I wasn't at school, I filled in. He paid me minimum wage for pumping gas and handling everyday tasks like patching tires, oil changes, lubes, and tune-ups. He appreciated that I was honest and reliable, and he taught me things that sharpened my skills. The work was pleasant. I was on my own and interacting with other people only superficially.

I mentioned during the interview that I didn't have tools. Mechanics are sometimes required to supply their own. Fortunately, that would not be an issue here. The dealership assigned each man a complete set, a multi-drawer affair on a rolling chassis holding scads of different devices. Few working men could have afforded one of these. If hired, I would be responsible for its contents. When I left the company an inventory would be taken, and I would have to pay for anything missing. Items damaged or broken while on the job were replaced at the dealer's cost. The mechanic had only to report them to his supervisor.

The employment manager reviewed the salary and benefits. With a little overtime I'd be earning more than twice what I was getting at Catalano's, which paid by the hour and offered no benefits. It seemed like a terrific opportunity.

The employment manager handed me off to the service manager, who supervised the garage and scheduled the repair work, a polite low-key guy named Rob. His would be the final decision. He said that my Army experience was especially valuable because I had been formally trained. Lots of applicants, he said, were fly-by-night mechanics, not learning particular skills until they needed to and then often in a half-assed way.

We took a tour. The operation was huge and first-class in every aspect, the biggest dealership I'd ever seen: offices everywhere; new car lot; used car lot holding easily a hundred vehicles packed in rows like sardines; showroom set up like a jewelry store staffed by salesmen wearing suits and ties standing around picking their teeth or schmoozing with potential buyers. . .everything outsized and spread over three acres. The garage held ten bays, distributed equally along both sides of the drive-through, each with a lift, and the floor ridiculously clean for a mechanic's workspace. In the end Rob asked what I thought of the operation, and I said it would be an honor to work there. He said he was glad to hear it because he was a man short and falling behind schedule. Everything, he said, is about customer service, and part of that was delivering exceptional repair work on time. If I wanted I could start the next day. I said I did and I could. We shook and returned to the office to fill out the paperwork. What little money I'd saved was nearly gone, and it was time I took some of the weight off Julie's shoulders.

I'd given Catalano's two weeks' notice before moving and said goodbye to Giovanni, Angel, Renato, the chef crew, and the happy hour regulars. Angel said, "Hell, youse is only moving to Sheepshead Bay, a few minutes on the D train. It ain't like Manhattan or some other foreign country at the end of the world where sensible people don't go." We laughed, and I said I'd be seeing him soon.

Julie and I and were married on a warm spring night. Neither of us was much for attending church, so we held a family meeting to decide the venue. The decision to hold the ceremony on the boardwalk was unanimous: three votes in favor, none opposed. I'd already asked Julie and Amy if they would consent to take my surname, and Amy if she would be my adopted daughter. I was thrilled when they agreed.

We hired an adoption attorney. There weren't any glitches because of Julie's tenacity and foresight. She had tracked down her estranged first husband and obtained a divorce shortly after I disappeared, which she already had been planning to do. Simultaneously, she gained sole custody of Amy. As part of the divorce agreement she relinquished any present and future demands for alimony or child support. That sealed the deal, and she and Amy emerged broke but free. There had been no ties or disagreements with the second husband. The split had been straightforward, both parties wanting out with as little fuss as possible.

A couple of months before the wedding I'd gone down to Catalano's after work. I purposely arrived during happy hour hoping to see Father Joe and ask if he would officiate at our nuptials. I was nervous, knowing he was important and might be too busy, or maybe just not want to be bothered, especially because Julie and I weren't Catholic and not getting married in church. But when I asked he clapped me on the shoulder and shook my hand and said he'd be honored. He bought me a drink, then asked the date. I said it was up to him, so long as it was a weekend. He took out a datebook and said May 10th. He could be free in the evening, say, for an eight o'clock ceremony. I thanked him and went to the kitchen where I gave Angel the place, date, and time of the ceremony. No gift, I reminded him, just his presence. When I went back to the bar Willie and Lenny each insisted on buying me a drink. I recruited them too, then Angel came out and bought me another. I was feeling no pain when I finally got home.

I had investigated when sunset would take place on May 10th. By coincidence it was exactly one minute past eight, just as the ceremony would be getting underway. From then on the available illumination would emanate from Nathan's Famous and nearby streetlamps lining the boardwalk.

I kept my eyes on Father Joe starting as soon as he arrived so as not to miss any cues he might direct our way. The sunlight diminished steadily as I continued to watch him, and as the daylight faded he turned strangely numinous, assuming an almost imperceptible glow that persisted even in moments when he ought to have been thrown into shadow. This effect gave him a holy, almost translucent appearance. The low surf, now invisible, gurgled and hissed in the encroaching darkness beyond, and swirling mist wrapped the streetlamps in haloes. The murmuring voices of curious onlookers seemed to rise up through the boards.

I felt a strange tingling sensation accompanied by a premonition that Father Joe was about to dissipate into the ether. At that moment Julie whispered that he looked pale and distracted, as if in a hurry to be off somewhere but not knowing how to say goodbye. We brushed it off because Father Joe had opened his Bible, and suddenly we were the center of attention. He was smiling graciously at everyone, about to tie Julie and me together forever.

Amy was her mother's bridesmaid, a ribbon in her hair and holding a bouquet of spring flowers, the same as Julie's. Angel stood beside me as best man. Willie and Lenny were the designated ushers and doubled as the bride's surrogate dads to give her away, one on each side, her arms looped through theirs. That was it. There was no one else, nor did there need to be. As we were milling around after the ceremony Angel approached Julie and kissed her on the cheek. He said to her, "Youse is a peach. If ever youse was to throw over this hillbilly stiff youse just married, come find me at Catalano's. I'd be happy to commit."

Father Joe died suddenly the following week. It happened during Thursday happy hour. Patrons reported that he turned his barstool around intending to stand, grabbed his chest, groaned, and toppled over. Renato phoned 911 practically as Father Joe hit the deck. Help arrived within minutes. It was no use, and the EMTs pronounced him dead on the spot.

The outpouring of grief was extraordinary for someone who officially wasn't even a parish priest. People came out of the woodwork, as the saying goes, from all over Brooklyn to pay respects at the Shrine Church of Our Lady of Solace on West 17th Street. And, of course, his scientific colleagues made a united showing from colleges, universities, and institutions throughout the region. His research accomplishments were highly regarded, as was his reputation as a collaborator and kindly mentor.

It was astonishing, truly, the impact his death

exerted on the entire borough and beyond, but Coney Island residents especially. Father Joe had been born and raised in Park Slope, and most of his family still lived in that neighborhood. He was interred there in Holy Cross Cemetery on Tilden Avenue alongside pre-deceased family members. The Bishop of Brooklyn himself stood graveside. He blessed the site and offered the eulogy, then said the Rite of Committal: *O God, by whose mercy the faithful departed find rest, bless this grave, and send your holy angel to watch over it. As we bury here the body of our brother, deliver his soul from every bond of sin, that he may rejoice in you with your saints forever. We ask this through Christ our Lord. Amen.*

Many mourners wept openly and loudly. At times it was difficult to hear the Bishop's words. Angel, Julie, and I stood together near the back of the crowd. I looked around and noticed a woman alone wearing a short black dress and heels and a black hat with a veil. She was blonde, her face was hidden, her shoulders shaking as if she might be weeping softly. I elbowed Angel and nodded slightly in her direction. He glanced over and whispered to me, "Yeah, I seen her already. Doctor Susie. I'd recognize them legs anywhere." Abruptly, she turned and left before the ceremony ended. We never saw her again.

Behind the bar at Catalano's, high above the tiers of bottles and atop the mirror behind them was an inconspicuous shelf perhaps eighteen inches wide. Since I had been working there it had held only a dusty crucifix, but now Renato stood on a ladder and pushed it to one side. Next to it he placed Father Joe's unfinished bottle of Glenfiddich single-malt scotch.

Never, he proclaimed, would another drink be poured from its mouth. Instead, he told us in so many garbled words, the bottle from this day forth would represent a permanent icon to the good Father's memory, and a reminder of his indomitable spirit. May he rest in peace. "Amen," said the resident barflies. "Amen," came the echo from the staff.

Chapter 12

————◆◆————

THE NEXT MAY AROUND the time of our first anniversary we bought a car. I had noticed a blue 1961 four-door Chevy Bel Air in the used car lot at the dealership. It had low mileage and good rubber and had never been wrecked. I put it on the lift and checked it out. As a show of loyalty we financed it through the dealership even though Julie's bank might have offered a slightly better rate. Amy had lobbied hard for a convertible. Eventually, I convinced her that without a garage it wasn't a good idea. Weather takes a toll on convertible tops, and breaking into a ragtop is absurdly easy, a thief needing just a sharp knife. Finally, for these reasons insurance would be more expensive. She relented, but emphasized it was only until we had a house of our own with a secure garage.

When school let out in June we took our first vacation, a road trip to Key West. As we were leaving the city Amy leaned forward from the backseat. "Are we going to stop in West Virginia to see my grandparents?"

After a moment I said, "No, it isn't a good idea." Then came the inevitable, why not. "Would you want to spend part of your vacation visiting your birth father or first stepfather?"

"No."

"This is the same sort of deal. Sometimes it's better to break completely from family members who make you unhappy, especially when you know the situation won't change."

"Are they still alive?'

"I don't know."

"Do you care?"

"Only in the sense that I hate to think that anyone I knew has died."

She sat back on the seat. "Okay, I understand."

We took our time, stopping along the way to see the sights. We spent a night in a motel in the Great Smoky Mountains of Tennessee because I wanted Julie and Amy to hear the whippoorwills calling at night, an eerie yet oddly comforting sound. I explained that whippoorwills and their near relatives are strange, mythical birds found on every continent except Antarctica. Bowing to a myth that dates back two millenniums, ornithologists placed them in the Goatsucker family. Myth has it that these birds, which are nocturnal and never seen in daylight, creep up on goats and sheep in the night and suckle from them. That particular teat then falls off, and the host animal providing the milk goes blind. Ancient Greeks believed this, and so still do some modern hillbillies. To me, the calls bring back memories of growing up in the mountains, a pleasant reminder of childhood summer nights. I was a little homesick, not for persons, but for place.

We continued south, taking in Charleston and Savannah. I told the girls about splitting firewood for Miz Henderson and Macie during my only other visit to Savannah, how I was given sandwiches and twenty dollars. We drove around looking for the neighborhood but couldn't find it. I omitted mention of Raymond and the drugs in front of Amy, although later told Julie the story, including Raymond being shot and killed. I said that I still thought about him and wondered whether I could have prevented his death by not giving him advice on thumbing rides. She snuggled up to me and said that it wasn't my fault, that no one can predict the future. Things like that just happen. I'd remember her words later when in the midst of the most devastating event of our lives.

We took a breather in St. Augustine to visit Marine Studios and watch the dolphins perform, then checked into a nearby motel and spent the afternoon at the beach. A day and a half later we reached Key West.

———————

Since last I saw them Josie and Arnold had moved in together and adopted a young Haitian girl who had been abandoned in Key West without any relatives or acquaintances; in fact, without anyone at all. No one even knew how she got there, and she was silent on the subject. Children's Services was about to scoop her up when Arnold and Josie came to the rescue. They had named her Silvia. She was Amy's age and equally precocious. With school out for the summer she was spending mornings with Arnold, a real estate agent, following him around as he showed properties to prospective clients. During afternoons she hung out in the resort's reception area, puttering around the office and running errands, like fetching Josie's coffee from Diner Shores, and even going to the pool by herself, where she splashed around under the watchful eyes of Ida and Junior from the bar.

Our greetings to Josie and Arnold were accompanied by handshakes and hugs all around. We introduced Amy by saying, please meet your uncles Josie and Arnold and your new cousin Silvia. The girls looked each over, and I saw mischief in their eyes. Amy said, "I always wanted a twin sister so there'd be two of me, but a cousin will do just fine."

Silvia piped up: "Daddy Arnold and I just sold a condo."

"Oh really?" Arnold said. "I thought it was me that sold it."

Silvia said, "Actually, you almost blew the deal. It would have tanked if I hadn't mentioned the powder room, which you forgot to tell them about. But never mind, you can make it up to me." She changed the subject. "I have two dads and no mom. Do you think that's weird?" She was looking at Amy when she spoke.

Amy picked up the cue. "Not so much. I have one of each and sometimes *that's* weird. Anyhow, who cares? It's whether you love each other that matters."

Silvia looked at the floor and stirred it around with her foot. She evidently wasn't through. "My daddies told me not to worry that I don't look like them or my other relatives. Daddy Josie says that differences in skin color are horseshit and don't mean squat, and genetics and gender are overrated. Right, Daddy?" She looked up at Josie.

"That's right, sweetie."

Julie laughed and said, "Oh god, another one!"

I said, "Well, Amy, let's put our stuff in the room then go look around. Want to see the aquarium? The six-toed cats at Hemingway's house?"

"I want to see the naked people by the pool," she said.

"I can show you that," said Silvia. "I go there all the time. We can go together, but I have to wear a swimsuit. My daddies don't allow me over there naked."

Amy said, "Tell me in advance: is it really, really weird?"

"Totally," Silvia said. "You have no idea."

I looked at Julie, who shrugged. "Okay," I said. "Everyone in swimsuits, and we hit the pool." We collected the key and went to our room to change.

"You're no fun!" Josie shouted at my back. "But check out the bar clientele."

––––––––––––

We took the girls to the pool. Silvia was nonchalant, Amy wide-eyed.

"I can't believe it! This is awesome!"

"Look at those two," Silvia whispered. "They'd probably look better with their clothes on."

Julie found a vacant chaise and stayed to watch the girls while I went to the bar. Josie's last comment had stimulated my curiosity. Sure enough, there sat not one surprise, but two. "Willie White Eyes and Lenny the Lurch!" I said, and wrapped my arms around one, then the other.

"Willie turned his bulk halfway. "Hey! How're youse doing? Sit wit us and have a drink." He waved, "Hey Ida and Junior, look who's came down from New York to hang out wit us!" Hugs accompanied by snide comments were exchanged across the bar.

"I'm here with my family." I pointed to Julie. "The little girl with Silvia is our daughter Amy."

"I heard you'd found each other and gotten together again," Ida said.

"Yeah, Julie and I got married. Talk about ser-endipity. Guess it was meant to be. I'll make your acquaintances and reacquaintances when they take a break from the pool." I said to Willie and Lenny "What are y'all doing in Florida in summer? I thought that when the weather heats up it was summers in Paradise North."

"That's true," Willie said, "but youse might say we're down here on business. Key West growed on me and Lenny ever since that first trip, and we plan to come back every winter for a few weeks. This time it's a business trip. Besides, it's nice here any time of year. The place is relaxing but has a lotta life. Wit the ocean breezes it's no hotter in summer than Brooklyn. And it's lively, right? Them pictures of tropical islands wit deserted beaches and waving palm trees, that ain't paradise. Youse can't have a good time and get laid where there ain't no people, for chrissakes. Which reminds me, when we—that's me and Lenny—call the escort service here in Key West the scheduler wants to know if we request female or male companionship." He barked a laugh. "Now, that's different! One time Lenny says to the dispatcher or scheduler or whatever he is, 'We desires two females, but check them good first 'cause we don't want no mistakes. Sometimes youse can't tell which is which when the merchandise arrives and their clothes is still on.'"

Lenny said, "Key West is great. Me and Willie, we're getting too old and lazy for hustling pussy offa barstools. Better to pay for it. There's no complications, right Willie?

"Yeah," Willie said. "And where in Brooklyn would we find palm trees? They'd freeze."

"Mario's Ristorante in Canarsie has palm trees outside the front door," Lenny said.

"Them is plastic," Willie said.

"Yeah, but Mario's trees don't freeze. I seen them covered wit snow, and they was still green."

Willie threw up his arms. "Jesus, Lenny, plastic don't freeze, *capisce?*"

I asked them, "Y'all stay here at the resort when visiting?"

Willie said, "Naw, we bought condos and hang out here for entertainment. Arnold, as youse probably knows, has a real estate license. Him and Josie went into business together as J & A Real Estate and Property Management. They manage our condos when we ain't here, rent them out to respectable people who don't trash a place, mostly gays. As a rule, gays is very respectful of other people's property. The rental return covers all our ownership expenses: taxes, association fees, J & A's management fees, everything. We basically vacation in Paradise South at bargain rates.

"But I gotta tell youse a weird a story. After buying our condos Josie remarks that now me and Lenny is conchs. Together, we say, *what?* Ain't that so, Lenny?" Lenny nodded. "We was prepared to be insulted until Josie explains that a 'conch' ain't only a snail that lives underwater in the ocean, it refers to someone who's a resident of Key West. Now, Josie says, as property owners we officially become citizens of the Conch Republic. You see, we was confused 'cause we don't understand him there for a minute. We seen one of them conchs over at the aquarium, the real kind. It stuck out its thing that looked like a big ugly toenail. Is it true, people eat them conchs?"

I said, "Sure. They pull the conch out of its shell then chop it up to make conch fritters, which are like tropical versions of clams fritters, and conch chowder, which is like clam chowder up north. Conchs and clams are related."

"I'll be goddamn. We didn't know," Willie said. "So, it took getting usta the idea that some schmuck introducing us as conchs don't necessarily mean we look like one, and so we let it slide instead of tap-dancing on his face."

"Right decision," I said. "It's meant as a compliment, as in, you're one of us now, part of a special tribe, a member of the exclusive Conch Republic. It's harmless stuff."

"Okay, 'cause on that conch we seen at the aquarium, the thing it stuck out of its shell and pointed at us looked like the nail of Lenny's big toe, the one on his club foot that no manicurist will touch, right Lenny?"

"Yeah, they take one look at it and run away."

"Anyhow," Willie said, "Arnold and Josie know everybody. Their business is going gangbusters, so to speak. I'm proud of them, and that little girl, Silvia, she's a peach. Smart? Christ, she scares me."

"You sound like a proud papa."

"Well, just between us, J & A was short of cash at startup, so I reach in my pocket for a little whip-out to help, not a loan, I say to them, but a piece of the action. We talk salaries and such when youse turns the corner. Meantime, we fly on my money and youse sweat. They say that's fine wit us, we'd be busting ass anyhow. So, I'm a silent partner. I got twenty-five percent ownership, and it's already paying off. Arnold works around the clock hustling new clients. Josie, he keeps his job here to pay their living expenses and pinches every penny of the new business till it screams for mercy. Plus, it's a great way to meet new clients, being the manager of this place. Josie drops a business card on them, then Arnold swoops in for the show-and-tell. A local lawyer, another gay guy, handles the legal stuff. A better arrangement I couldn't imagine." He lit a cigar and waved to the bartenders for another round.

"Here's a example of how it pays to be a inside investor. When this developer, see, is building a new condo complex me and Lenny buy two units for our future winter retirement. Arnold and Josie, they got a finger on the pulse of the real estate market here in Key West. Jungle drums tell them the developer is running a little short on cash 'cause certain subcontractors is starting to bitch about not being paid. As a result, the units go up for sale unofficially before any formal announcement. Arnold, representing me and Lenny, makes a crazy low-ball offer of cash, no banks or nuttin, just greased cash hand to hand, get it? The site is still under construction, meaning there's a little risk on our part, but what the hell.

"The developer is so impressed by how quick Arnold and Josie move he gives them exclusive sales rights for six months, and they open the bidding. Guess what? They sell out in three before even the palm trees is installed! Real ones, I should add. Our company pockets the commission, the lawyer we use snaps up most of the closings, the developer pays off his bills and takes a nice payday, and everybody's happy. Turns out me and Lenny coulda sold our units almost immediately and made a fifty percent profit before the paint is dry. But enough about us, wassup witchuse? We know youse still ain't washing dishes in Coney Island, and obviously youse ain't fixing leaky faucets down here. Angel said something about being a mechanic?"

"I had to grow up and get a big-boy job. With a family to help support I had to make something of myself, you know, 'be somebody.' I went back to auto mechanics, which is steady, reliable, and comes with good pay and benefits. Julie works too, at a bank. She's just been made a trust officer handling and investing money for rich people and setting up their offspring to be trust-fund babies. She has a bachelor's degree in finance. And Amy is as scary-smart as you say Silvia is. So, all is good. We live in Sheepshead Bay, but you know this, so you're bullshitting me. Y'all were Julie's dads at the wedding, and we chatted at Father Joe's funeral. Nothing's really changed since then. Our next goal is to buy a house, but that's off in the hazy future. What would be perfect is a place in Sheepshead

Bay. We really like the neighborhood. We're close to schools, work, and so forth. Good location. Hey, here comes my family."

I said to Amy, "These are your uncles Willie and Lenny. You remember him from the wedding. Don't hug them, you're wet. Shake their hands. And here's Julie."

Willie took off his sunglasses and said as if seeing them for the first time, "Lookit, Lenny! My god, they're beautiful!" Then to Julie, "What're youse hanging out wit a bum like him for? Youse coulda married a sweet handsome guy wit class, somebody like me." Everyone laughed, Willie heartiest of all, a two-day growth sandpapering that heavy face with a cigar sticking out of it, the mosaic brown and white eyes seemingly focused nowhere but surreptitiously all-seeing.

Julie wondered aloud if Amy and Silvia would be safe if she needed to leave them alone to use the bathroom or wanted to have a drink with us. Ida said, "Those little girls couldn't be safer. Junior and I know the signals from every category of pervert, including pedophiles. We're looking over there all the time, and if we miss something—which is highly unlikely—all they need to do is yell and one of us is there, probably both of us. Those kids are wise in the ways of the world, lots more aware than I was at their age. They can swim like fish, so no lifeguarding required. Leave the rest to us. Any drownings will result from Junior and me holding a perv underwater until he stops blowing bubbles."

Willie added, "Me and Lenny can be backups, considering we're usually on duty witchuse and Junior. I'm a floater and maybe could contribute, but Lenny wit his scrawny ass, it might be another life to save. He's built like a sinker. Can youse swim, Lenny?

"I dunno. I never tried."

Willie seemed astonished. He took the cigar out of his mouth and said, "As a kid youse never put on a swimsuit in summer and went to the pool?"

It was Lenny's turn to be surprised. "Why would I do that?"

———————

We had a terrific time. We took Silvia with us and strolled the streets of Key West seeing the sights, then lunch, sometimes at Diner Shores, and happy hour at the bar while Amy and Silvia played in the pool. Afterward, showers, out to dinner, and adults back at the bar while the girls watched TV in our room. One afternoon Willie came along on our escapades to see the cat circus in Mallory Square at sunset, where domestic cats have been trained to jump through hoops and perform other tricks.

Willie had become increasingly interested in Julie's educational background and her responsibilities at the bank. She noticed too, considered it unusual, and wanted my take. I said, "He's probably planning a heist. Be suspicious if he asks you for floor plans and armored car schedules."

She said, "No, seriously, he has something up his sleeve. I'm curious to learn what it could be. He's bound to show his cards before we leave for home."

She was prescient. Two nights before we were scheduled to drive back to New York Willie set up dinner at La-Te-Da. Present were Willie, Lenny, Amy,

Julie, me, Arnold, Josie, and Silvia. Willie sat at the head of the table. Dinner conversation was the usual small talk: the status of local business, how the resort was faring, that sort of thing. After dessert Willie ordered a round of dessert wines. At that point Amy and Silvia split for upstairs to watch the drag show. At their age it was illegal to be there, but an exception was made, and they were destined for premium seats at the bar and virgin daiquiris.

Willie said he had something to say to us and that he was calling an official meeting. He said, "I've decided to retire and split time between here and Coney Island. Lenny is doing the same. We done our time, literally in some cases." That brought a laugh. "What I'm about to tell youse has to do wit me and my finances. Lenny is making his own plans. So, I had two business careers. I was already in the wiseguy profession when I later picked up the parking lot gig, the second a direct result of the first. I won't go into details and take the fifth, 'cause as they say I might incriminate myself." He smiled around his cigar. "Me and my two brothers, we never married or had kids, so we now got a situation of what to do wit our real estate and loot stashed away in various banks when we croak. I'm in the process of selling my third of the parking lot to Frankie and Larry. They're younger and want to keep working. Hell, they got nuttin else to do. That'll toss more scratch that I don't need onto my pile. So, what to do wit it? Well, I feel like spreading some around, know what I mean?

"I've give the matter a lotta thought, and here's what I conclude. My brothers, they don't need to inherit from me. They got plenty. They'll probably never get outta Coney Island even for a vacation, maybe never retire. Them two, they think they need a passport to leave Brooklyn. Larry will probably collapse of old age while sitting in his booth. Frankie? I predict he dies in his office and falls face-down on top of a spreadsheet. Hold on a minute while I check my notes." He opened a small notebook taken from his jacket pocket and held it in front of him, shifting it different distances from his face. "I can't read the goddamn thing. Wait." He set it down, took off his sunglasses, and put on a pair of reading glasses. "Funny, right? Willie White Eyes needs reading glasses. Mister Scary Mobster, Mister Bigtime Wiseguy, hasta get cheaters from the drugstore. Ha! Don't mention it to none of my colleagues from Queens. They might conclude I'm blind and helpless and consider fitting me wit cement shoes. Anyhow, youse four and the kids and Ida and Junior is gonna be my new family. Oh, and Angel, of course. Can't leave him out. I love that spic rat-bastid, but for the life of me don't know why. He's such a smartass."

Willie shifted in his chair and lit a fresh cigar. "I been on the phone lots wit Frankie lately. He knows some accounting stuff I needed to learn about, such as how to give money away and not pay taxes on it." He picked up his notebook and adjusted his glasses.

"So, Julie, I'm putting youse at the head of this parade. Youse is a trust officer at a bank. When youse gets home start setting up some trusts, like college funds for Silvia and Amy so's they can go to any college they want and not have to pay a nickel. The bank where youse work has trust lawyers. Maybe use them, but Frankie advises setting up family trusts in Delaware where it's cheaper and more convenient than New York or Florida, and 'cause the trustees have more authority about how the funds can be managed and distributed. It don't matter to me either way. I'm paying all the expenses to set the table, so do what youse believe is best. Make wills for me and for Lenny, if he wants one, and advise us how to distribute what's left, that's the cash and real estate holdings. Put my holdings in a trust, if that's best, and youse and me will discuss its final distribution after I croak. And ast Lenny if he wants to contribute to any of these trusts from the start, like for Amy and Silvia, okay? What he does is his own business.

"Meantime, youse and this former dishwasher youse married start looking around Sheepshead Bay at houses for sale. Take the time to find exactly what youse want. I'll buy it for youse, wit either cash or a mortgage, whichever is most financially beneficial. Be sure it has a yard wit some nice trees. Kids need to grow up knowing what a tree looks like, right? Frankie also says there's a scam called a house trust youse might consider. Maybe drop the new property in it for tax and inheritance purposes. No doubt youse know about these things.

"I'll give youse my bank account numbers, copies of deeds, and whatever limited power of attorney is necessary to transfer the funds to the bank where youse work so's the bills can be paid. I don't need no overpaid bankers coming after my kneecaps 'cause they think I'm stiffing them. Line up the paperwork

I need to sign, and I'll let youse know where I am at any moment so's I'm available: Coney Island, Key West, various racetracks. Who knows? I'm retired, remember? Maybe them suits back in Sheepshead Bay will give youse a promotion and a raise for bringing in this business, if youse decides to keep it there.

"Set up a trust for Angel where he gets a regular payout, say monthly, to supplement his income. He'll probably never leave Catalano's and be scrubbing pots when he's a geezer. But I don't want him ending up on the streets, and I hate to think of him living in that fleabag hotel next door to petty thieves and junkie hookers wit snarled hair and attitude hanging off their addictions. He needs to upgrade his residence. Work it out so's he inherits when me, Willie White Eyes, cashes in his chips. Julie, youse and stump-jumper here should be trustees for Angel's trust 'cause youse live just a subway stop up the line if something goes wrong, God forbid. Determine that if Angel can't handle money then youse continue the regular payouts instead of a lump sum so's he's always walking around wit a little bread in his pockets and not fall on tough times. Arnold and Josie is too far away to serve in this capacity. Anyhow, they won't have the time to spare. They're gonna be balls to the walls making me and Lenny and theirself rich.

"For Josie and Arnold, figure how to turn over my part of J & A to them, again so's it screws the fucking IRS, maybe make it part of their trust. Do whatever's best. I want these two living large on their own hustle quick as possible so's me and them have loose change jingling for which we snap up some tasty local real estate investments as they become available and they manage my share. I put them on notice already: I expect to be first to the action, like we was to me and Lenny's condos. Only losers wait in line and suck hind tit.

"Set up trusts for Ida and Junior, no regular pay-outs but lump sums at my death. Finally, tell them two little girls from now on to call me and Lenny *Nonno*, which is Italian for grandpa. To youse four I'll be Uncle Willie White Eyes. It'll make us seem more family, but informally in real life just plain Willie, as I always been. Now, how's about a round of Irish coffees to celebrate? Waiter!"

We sat there stunned. Julie started to cry. "I can't believe this," she said. She got out of her chair and went to hug Willie, then the rest of us followed her lead. Arnold and Josie were weeping too. I held it together but not entirely dry-eyed. That someone could be so kind seemed a miracle, and that he had thought everything out, even attempting to predict the consequences of his largess, was amazing. Anyone thinking of Willie as an ignoramus was badly mistaken. It goes to show that you can't always judge someone by appearances or regional dialect. Here was at least one New York wiseguy of generous spirit and truly with a heart of gold.

Just then Amy and Silvia showed up looking startled. Silvia said, "What's wrong with you guys? Is everything okay?"

"Everything's fine, sweetie," Josie said. "We're just very happy is all."

Amy rolled her eyes and said, "Ignore it Silvia.

Adults are so weird. But we're happy too, because we decided something important. Want to hear it?"

"Sure," Julie said. The girls put their arms around each other's waists.

Silvia said, "We decided not to be cousins. We're going to be sisters instead."

Josie jumped to his feet. "Well, this deserves a round of applause, everyone! Don't you agree?" And we stood and clapped while the girls took a bow.

Chapter 13

———◦◦———

THE NEXT SUMMER ANGEL and Giovanni came to Key West for a visit. We had coordinated their arrival to coincide with our second vacation there. Willie and Lenny would be around too, and Arnold, Josie, Silvia, Ida, and Junior, of course. Amy and Silvia were excited at the prospect of spending a full two weeks together. All in all, it would make for a nice reunion, and everyone was looking forward to it. Angel reported that Giovanni had gotten used to flying and now was reasonably calm, except during takeoff and landing. The final leg in the small commuter plane from Miami would be a first and probably unnerve him, but on the whole he was getting better. Baby steps, Angel said.

My family had spent the intervening year productively. Julie had nearly finished setting up Willie's trusts and had been promoted to assistant trust manager at the bank. Amy was crushing her schoolwork, never scoring any grade less than A. Meanwhile, Rob had recognized my mechanical skills and was assigning me the more difficult repair jobs, which also were the most interesting. Julie and I had found a house on a quiet cul-de-sac with a two-car garage and bought a convertible to fill the vacant bay. After Julie and the realtor negotiated a final price, Willie ordered the title put in Julie's and my name and paid the entire amount in cash, including closing costs. Our lives were perfect, and now we were in Paradise South kicking back with our best friends.

Amy and Silvia were splashing in the pool while Julie relaxed in a chaise nearby reading a novel plucked from the resort's library. I was sitting at the bar with Willie and Lenny, Willie in the middle. He turned to me and said, "Me and Lenny, we're flush from our investments. We sometimes take a limo up to Hialeah, blow a coupla thou each on the ponies, and don't even feel the pinch. It's just whip-out, know what I mean? We're living large. Life in Paradise South couldn't be better.

"So, to spread the good cheer we offer to buy Angel a condo down here so's he can retire and hang out wit us in this fine weather sitting at bars in the open air and busting chops like retirees oughta. Enjoy life, right? We tell him this when last we fly to New York to see old pals. This discussion happens last winter when it's freezing out. Catalano's is dead, so we ast Renato to go fetch Angel, that we want to talk to him. Angel, he saunters out of the kitchen wearing them ridiculous gloves. Youse seen spics and how they strut. They remind me of them fighting roosters that walk that way to make other roosters think their balls is bigger. Sit, we tell him, we got a proposition for youse, which we tell him about.

"He says to us that he ain't interested, but thanks for thinking of him, that he don't want to be indebted and have his kneecaps broke for not paying a bill or something. This last is a joke, of course. Then we change the offer. I say, suppose we buy another condo in our complex and youse lives there free in the winter? We rent it the rest of the year and come out even, no sweat. You ain't beholding to nobody. Don't believe us, have Josie open his books and show youse the numbers next time youse comes down to Florida. And in case youse ain't been outside lately, Paradise South is looking a helluva lot better right now than Paradise North. I jerk my thumb at the window, which youse can't see through 'cause sleet is froze to it. Know what he says? He says he'll think about it!"

Willie waved his hand in the air for emphasis. "Spics! Who can understand them? What are me and Lenny missing? We try to be good Samarisons, distribute a little bread we don't need over the waters, so to speak. Ast Lenny." He turned to Lenny. "Ain't that right, Lenny?'

"Yeah," said Lenny. "A guy can only eat so much bread then it ain't satisfying no longer. It's filling, right? Me, when I eat too much bread I get a stomach ache."

Willie turned back to me and spread his arms in confirmation. "There youse has it."

Angel and Giovanni arrived at the resort the next afternoon and checked into their room. Angel found me in the bar talking to Ida and Junior. After the usual greetings Angel said, "Youse shoulda been there when Hercules and Jan was reunited. They run into one another's arms other like lost lovers, all smiles and hugs and kisses on the cheek. Then they bust out crying, the two of them. Jan sobs out something in polack, Hercules dittos in wop, and they disappear arm and arm into the kitchen. Ten minutes they're yelling at each other. It's like old times. Looks like they'll be bitter friends to the end."

None of us realized that Willie and Lenny's offer to buy Angel a condo was about to be revived. The trigger proved to be the bartenders' schedule, or rather, the lack of one. Ida and Junior rarely took time off. Maybe a week during off-season to visit family. The routine was wearing on them. They went to Josie and told him they needed a backup. After all, they argued, they weren't costing the resort much, considering tips composed most of their income. He thought a minute and agreed. But how to find someone compatible? Or, as Josie phrased it, where do we get somebody dumb enough to put up with your shit? They told him they had an idea. They proposed conscripting Angel and training him.

"Brilliant!" Josie said. "Do it, sweeties!"

The next afternoon Angel and I were alone at the bar. Angel figured correctly that the guys had told me he'd rejected their offer either to buy him a condo or buy another for themselves where he could live rent-free during the winter. He said he felt bad about hurting their feelings when they were trying to be generous. "I love them two dago mooks. Youse knows this. But sometimes they don't think too clear.

They believe I can retire and sit on my ass like they do, but I ain't them. I'm still a working stiff and usually broke. I earn just enough to survive week to week. Youse understands this, but they don't."

Ida, who had been eavesdropping, said, "Not anymore. Scoot your ass over to our side of the bar."

"What?" Angel said.

"You heard her," said Junior. "You're going to be a bartender."

"A bartender? *Me?* He placed his palm on his chest then looked my way accusingly. "Whose idea is this? Youse is squeezing my onions, right?"

"Hey, this is the first I heard it," I said.

"He's telling the truth," Ida said, "and we aren't joking. You've been loafing here too long. Junior and I came up with the idea, and Josie agreed. We haven't had a day off in memory and need a backup, someone reasonably reliable and sober so we can rotate out and take a breather occasionally."

"You'll be surprised how good the tips are," Junior said. "Now, come around the bar and let's get started. We have to whip you into shape before tourist season so you're not slammed. Besides the usual mixed drinks there's maybe a couple of dozen what Ida and I call 'fairy charms' you'll need to learn. Those are the colorful ones with tiny umbrellas, very popular and expensive. The flocking flagrant fruits adore them. Hey, try saying that really fast. Anyhow, trust us, you'll love this job. Ida will kick your ass if you don't learn fast enough. Me, I'll probably pinch it."

Ida said, "Yeah, and what the hell, you're halfway there. You already know how to wash dishes."

Angel chugged the remainder of his beer and threw his hands in the air. "Why not? I hadn't planned on spending the winter in Fruitcake South, but now that I am I better ast Willie and Lenny about room arrangements. They're gonna shit when they show up at happy hour and spot me behind the bar. They'll think I'm robbing the place and be pissed 'cause I didn't include them."

I asked him later if he wasn't going home to collect his stuff, and what about the little Cuban girl and his friends back there.

"I don't own nuttin worth the cost of a plane ticket. Manny can give it away to the bums and junkies. When I save a few tips I'll go to the thrift shop. Friends? I got more friends here than there. The Cuban girl? I ain't seen her in a while. I was stopgap to her until something better happened along. She found a Cuban guy who walks around wit wads of whip-out and could understand her Spanish. I think he's a drug dealer. Youse should know by now that the secret to staying single is to be a loser." He laughed. "And the scam works best when youse is sincere about it."

I said, "But now you have a terrific job in a great location. Some chick is going to think you're a catch. She'll have images of babies and white picket fences dancing in her head, and you'll capitulate and end up like the rest of the suckers."

"Stop already," he said. "Youse is scaring me."

It was on the third morning of Angel's bartending career that tragedy struck our little group. The bar hadn't yet opened when Jan rushed in wailing and yelling in Polish. He pointed back toward the resort and led the three of them to Diner Shores where a subdued crowd had gathered outside. They pushed through and found Giovanni lying on the floor in the dining area. Ida felt his pulse, then looked up at the others and shook her head. Nonetheless, Junior scurried to the phone and called 911, but the EMTs merely confirmed Ida's conclusion. For reasons of protocol the body was taken to the hospital so that the coroner could process it legally, then release it to a mortuary.

Giovanni and Angel had been sharing a room, although Angel's residence there had become temporary because Willie and Lenny had instructed Arnold to start shopping for a condo they were intent on buying him. Angel accepted the offer graciously this time, thrilled to have his own place paid for free and clear, although he'd be responsible for expenses and upkeep. Still, he wasn't going to let Willie off easy. He jokingly said that because wiseguys can't be trusted he was ordering a set of those hard plastic knee protectors that baseball catchers wear, that you never know when a moving length of iron pipe might suddenly appear in his path.

Giovanni had freaked out when Angel told him he was staying in Key West. Who would accompany him home? To comfort him Angel capitulated. When Giovanni's vacation ended he would take him home to New York using the remaining half of his round-trip ticket and deliver him to Coney Island, then come right back. Willie and Lenny were paying his expenses for the return trip to Key West. Angel had phoned Renato with this information while also announcing his resignation at Catalano's, asking that the owners be notified in his behalf and to please look after Greg. Giovanni's sudden death now required a follow-up call with the news and that Willie and Lenny would be delivering the urn containing Giovanni's ashes to Catalano's on their next trip north.

Giovanni had no living family, at least none anyone knew about. Standing in locally were Jan, Angel, Willie, Lenny, Arnold, and Josie backed by Julie, me, Ida, and Junior. In Coney Island was the ownership of Catalano's and the restaurant staff. Willie and Lenny stepped up and volunteered to cover funeral expenses. Josie telephoned a mortuary, which sent its crew to fetch the body from the hospital and store it, and to arrange a viewing and cremation. Angel gave Giovanni's tux to the funeral home with instructions to dress him in it. There would be a viewing for anyone who cared to attend, but no service.

Angel took Giovanni's death especially hard. As he'd once said, the old man had been like an grandfather to him, and it was clear that Giovanni reciprocated those feelings of closeness. Jan was also distressed. However tumultuous their relationship appeared to others, it had been based on admiration, respect, and the mutual love of food preparation.

———————

Ida, Junior, and Angel were getting the bar ready to open while Willie and Lenny perched impatiently on their regular stools. Angel remarked that Giovanni's dying in Key West had been tragic.

"Did I hear you say 'tragic?'" Ida apparently said.

Angel exploded. "Don't piss on my parade wit that college girl bullshit! It ain't funny!"

"I'm sorry, I didn't mean it to be funny, just that 'tragic' isn't a word in your everyday vocabulary. What do you mean by it?"

"I mean it's a fucking goddamn shame Hercules died down here 'cause he's so out of his element. Better he croaks in Catalano's in the act of yelling at another Sicilian waiter who's been working there long as him. And he shoulda been wearing his tux, not them loud tropical threads wit his chicken legs sticking out. It don't seem right. That's what I mean."

Junior said, "I agree with him, Ida. Put that way, it's tragic."

Ida stopped rearranging bottles and said to Angel, "You figure his heart gave out?"

Angel said, "I finger the perpetrator to be a change of diet that maybe triggered the heart. There's two possibilities. Number one, Hercules conks out from eating Jan's polack food, which is too foreign for his delicate wop stomach. Number two, Hercules cooks up some lasagna for himself and Jan sprinkles parsley on it when Hercules ain't looking. Culinary mistakes can be deadly." He started to cry.

Lenny said, "Don't do that, Angel. Youse will upset me and Willie. Youse knows how little it takes to make wiseguys cry. We're very sensitive to the pain of others."

"Unless they're the target, he means," Willie said. And as Ida later told me, sure enough, within seconds those two were in full teardrop mode. What would I have done? Probably stayed dry-eyed owing to my Scots-Irish hillbilly heritage, to which Ida had previously alerted me, and that I knew Giovanni only casually.

The funeral home agreed to hold the ashes in an urn. Willie and Lenny would eventually deliver them to Catalano's, where a final resting place had already been decided: they were destined for the shelf above the bar alongside the crucifix and Father Joe's bottle of scotch. From his ladder Renato would no doubt contribute one of his unique homilies.

Chapter 14

AMY BECAME ILL. SHE started losing her balance and falling. She had chronic headaches and intermittent episodes of violent vomiting that came on suddenly, seemingly unassociated with a faulty digestive system. Julie skipped a day of work and took her to the pediatrician, who expressed concern and referred us to the oncology department of our local hospital. The thought that Amy might have cancer was more than worrisome, it was terrifying.

The appointment was a week away, and during that brief interim Amy's symptoms worsened. Two days before the scheduled examination her pain became so severe that we took her to the emergency room where she was admitted and sedated. Julie and I were prepared to stay the night, but the ER staff advised going home and getting some sleep, that nothing would be done diagnostically until the next day when the full staff came on duty.

I went to work the next morning and told Rob the

situation. He said to take what time I needed, that his prayers and the dealership's were with us. Julie went directly to the hospital. She didn't call with any updates, so I worked a full shift and went home. Julie was there and said that tests were still being run. I showered, and we went to the hospital.

Amy was awake but very weak. She looked small and pale against the white sheets. I held her hand and started to cry, which started Julie crying. Amy said "Hey, you guys, don't cry. It's going to be okay." We did our best to stop, but it wasn't easy. When she fell asleep we went to the cafeteria and tried to choke down some food. Amy was still sleeping when we returned to her room, but visiting hours were over, and we had to leave.

Early the next morning the hospital called and said the doctor wanted to meet with us. We were to go to the nurses' station on Amy's floor. The duty nurse would summon the doctor, who was expecting us, and that afterward we could visit Amy.

The doctor took us into a small office and sat us down. "I have very bad news," he said, "and it would be unfair to sugar-coat the probable outcome. Your daughter has a pediatric-type diffuse high-grade glioma. In plain English, a malignant and aggressive type of brain tumor found most commonly in post-adolescents. The prognosis? Less than five percent of patients survive beyond two years. Realistically, median survival is nine to eighteen months. We'll do our best to beat those odds, of course. However, please understand that much of the effort will be palliative, damping down Amy's pain and keeping her as comfortable as we can." He explained that there are several types of gliomas. Some respond positively to therapy, but Amy's was not one of them. He said, "Our hospital staff is highly trained and capable, but only a miracle can save your daughter. I'm truly sorry."

Julie collapsed against me, and we both broke down. Dissolved might be a better description. How could this be happening? Amy was the perfect daughter, the three of us a perfect family. In that instant our world imploded, hurling us into entropic chaos. No treatment would alter the trajectory and change the outcome; there could be no collecting the shards and fitting them back together. Medical specialists had decreed Amy's fate. We could only stay the course and be there for her.

The doctor then explained the treatment regimen, but we barely listened so intense was our grief. We heard his voice fade in and out; certain words such as "radiation" and "chemotherapy" possessed vague meaning. As I recalled afterward, he mentioned possible surgery, but scans to date already were revealing the tumor's rapid spread. Surgery could never excise it all, and the remaining cells would continue to proliferate, spread, and coalesce into new tumorous tissue. I tried hard to focus on what he was saying, knowing Julie had disappeared into her grief. Treatment would start immediately. Amy would be an inpatient and hospitalized initially. When she could become an outpatient and go home depended on her response to the therapies, which themselves were debilitating, and to how the tumor responded.

Amy's symptoms had presented just a short time before and were progressing relentlessly. The effects were happening before our eyes, and the swiftness of her decline was heartbreaking. We could only stand by helplessly and watch. Amy had lost all appetite and was visibly shrinking. Severe headaches and frequent bouts of vomiting sapped what little of her energy remained. The ataxia was worsening. She was falling more often, and her arms and legs were covered in bruises. Recently, she had begun suffering seizures of frightening violence as the expanding tumor occluded more of her brain.

Amy never rallied sufficiently to become an outpatient. Julie and I took what time we could from our jobs to be there. We read her stories and held her hand. Sometimes we watched a movie together on TV. Mostly, we tried not to fall apart in her presence and when alone not discuss her sunken features, the radiation-induced baldness, the ever-present pain in her eyes. Either of us gladly would have taken her place.

One of us always tried to be there for chemotherapy sessions and stay to support her through the vomiting and dry heaves that followed. The feeling of helplessness was excruciating. Julie and I were losing weight too. The thought of eating brought only apathy and the monotony of chewing and swallowing food you don't want but know you need. We lost the capacity for laughter; happiness seemed a foreign place. I suppose this was part of anticipating death's finality, the passive resignation that accompanies losing your sense of self in a loved one's fate, the agony of waking up and plodding through the day;

of simply brushing your teeth, tying your shoes. The constant battle with inertia. Every act felt mundane and superfluous.

Silvia called Amy at the hospital every night at seven o'clock, and they talked until Amy became too exhausted. The conversations were becoming noticeably shorter until after two months they stopped. Amy was too sick to focus, the pain too great. She seemed to have given up. Indeed, there were no reasons for optimism, and continuing to live was only prolonging her agony.

The guys at the dealership were wonderful. When Rob sensed how badly things were going he told me to take whatever time I needed. When I apologized for not pulling my weight on the schedule, he did a remarkable thing. He went into the locker room, changed from his office clothes into overalls, and took my place underneath the lift. He instructed his secretary, who had worked there for nearly twenty years, to take over the scheduling and meet him at lunchtime to review the upcoming jobs, which he would continue to assign as usual, but for the time being from the work floor instead of sitting at his desk.

And then a quiet, unassuming guy named Alfie, a Brooklyn native, stepped up too. He was single, and his passion was fishing. Every year he took his two weeks of vacation, and he and his cousins went north to the Thousands Islands on the Saint Lawrence River where they fished for smallmouth bass and muskellunge and drank beer. This year he'd canceled out so as not to leave his bay vacant when the mechanics' room was already short a man. When I thanked him, he said, "Aw, hell, I can always go fishing. I'm happy to do it."

Amy had been in the hospital four months. One evening during our regular visit she said, "It hurts so much. I'm going to die, I know that. Please don't be sad. Tell Silvia and the rest of our relatives I'll see them on the other side. Maybe Father Joe and Nonno Giovanni will be there, and they'll recognize me. I want you guys to know that wherever I end up I'll always love you."

"Oh honey!" Julie said. She got on her knees and leaned her forehead on the edge of the bed. Amy reached over and touched her hair. She was crying too, and then so was I.

———————

Amy died in the night, and the nurses' station called to tell us. It wasn't unexpected, of course, but still a shock. Amy had been Julie's lifeblood and my conscience. How is it possible that such things happen? How could a perfect ethereal being suddenly vanish? We were nothing without her, two souls adrift. We had needed her to complete us.

I hired a jeweler to fashion two heart-shaped gold lockets about the size of a nickel strung on sturdy gold chains. I told him that hinges and clasps weren't necessary because the lids were to be sealed shut. When he called and told me they were finished I took some of Amy's ashes to his store, filled each locket with a tiny scoop, and instructed him to seal them. The engraving on Julie's said *Beloved Daughter* on one side and *Amy* on the other; Silvia's had *Beloved Sister* and *Amy*. As for me, Amy had long ago engraved herself into my heart. That's where she would nestle always, and I needed no other reminder.

———————

We took Amy's ashes to Key West and scattered them in the Atlantic Ocean at the southernmost point. We gave Silvia her locket, and she said she would never take it off, not ever. Our friends gathered for the occasion. It was a day of great sadness and good fellowship. They were now our only family, and we needed them badly.

But that, of course, was not the end. Amy was always with Julie and me in spirit. When children die you remember them at the age they were and fantasize how they might have turned out, how they might have looked and acted, put in their absent mouths the words of your own hopes and expectations. Julie and I do this all the time, especially when we're mellowed out by a few drinks. Would Amy have been an ER doctor? A college professor? A stay-at-home mother? How would the jewel of our lives, that crystalline presence, have reflected the sun as an adult? Then we go to bed and awake in the morning sad and dejected and a little angry at ourselves for playing this game, knowing the vacuity of conjecture, the hopelessness of unending grief.

Chapter 15

THE YEARS SLIPPED PAST. Julie had been promoted to head of the trust department at the bank, and I was now service manager at the dealership, Rob having retired. I went to work in a jacket and tie instead of overalls. From the start I tried to make the transition seamless, and it seems to have worked. I keep my relations with the guys in the bays professional and cordial, and when I had to name a head mechanic to replace myself I chose Alfie, who deserved it in every respect.

Each summer Julia and I spend two weeks at Ocean Shores Resort. Silvia had started high school and was thinking of going to college in New York, maybe Columbia or NYU. We told her that she would be welcome to move in with us and live in Amy's old room if she wanted, that she was our daughter too.

It was during one of these vacations, and I was sitting

at the bar alongside Willie and Lenny. The time of day was late afternoon. I believe Julie was in our room reading, although I don't recall exactly. We were all going gray. Even Angel's curly tresses had traces of white. Willie leaned against the back of his stool and said, "At first I busted Lenny's balls for not doing any financial planning. Then I remembered, Lenny's a dumbass. Also, he ain't got any relations, so his line ends wit him. My line ends too when me and my brothers croak, but the difference is I got family responsibilities, namely all of youse. Lenny don't, so why should he care?" He turned slightly toward Lenny. "Youse don't care, and youse is happy, right?"

"I don't give a rat's ass," Lenny said, "and was I any happier I couldn't hardly stand it."

"See?" Willie said. "What'd I tell youse? And why shouldn't he be? Julie set him up wit a investment portfolio she manages and cuts him a monthly check he cashes at the bank on Duvall Street. Then fast as possible he blows the wad on booze, cigars, sirloins, hookers, and horses. Sometimes he needs advances, but what the hell. The arrangement works perfect for him. Josie covers the management expenses for both of us: the light bills, taxes, bar tabs here at the resort, and so forth out of our separate accounts, all the bullshit we don't want to be bothered wit, right Lenny?

"Youse is right, Willie. Them details is aggravating."

"Do I need remind all of youse that this is Paradise South?" He was talking, of course, to Lenny and me and also to Angel, Ida, and Junior. "A typical day for me and Lenny starts wit breakfast at Diner Shores around nine or so. We bring along the *Daily News* and the *Daily Racing Form*, which arrive from New York on our doorsteps each morning in the wee hours. Josie has found a local bakery that makes a pretty decent bagel and passable cheese Danish. Maybe not so good as what Cohen's Bakery on West 16th Street in Coney Island dishes out, but passable, and Jan picks them up fresh on his way to work. They go terrific wit that dark Cuban coffee. Over a second cup and a cigar we come up to speed on news from New York and peruse the racing sheet, taking notes of bets we need to make. Breakfast over, we go to Josie's office and phone our bookies back in Brooklyn.

"By then it's eleven or so, maybe even twelve, and the bar is open, so we toddle over, strip off the clothes, and mount our usual stools on the east side facing the morning sun. We adjust our shades and proceed to renew our golden tans. We lay back, me so the belly creases stretch out and get some color. Even Lenny's Famous has acquired a glow around the ears, or where the ears would be if a trouser snake had them.

"Sometimes on weekends Silvia stops by. She ain't bothered by her *nonnos* splayed out naked. She's usta us. Gotta hand it to Josie and Arnold for raising her right. This kid is ready for life, I gotta tell youse. And she's a trip. When there's a special kind of a fish or sea creature that goes on display at the aquarium she's right there, and sometimes she drags us, her *nonnos*, over to look at the thing too. Me and Lenny, we got annual passes.

"The other day some fish laid eggs in its aquarium. It's a little purple and yellow fish, real pretty. She shows us how it dashes about blowing water on its eggs to keep away algae and parasites that might kill the babies inside. I ast is that the mother fish. She says no, it's the father, and we need to watch him carefully and pay attention to how hard he works and what a good dad he is, that he doesn't leave all the responsibility for the woman like deadbeat wiseguys usually do. Lenny says later in the bar, 'Silvia got us there, Willie. Stick and run, that's us.' Then she tells us she might be a marine biologist someday. Numbnuts Lenny says in his next life he wants to be one too. Silvia tells him that's unlikely 'cause he's too low in the, uh. . . .I can't think of the word."

"Evolutionary scale?" Ida said.

"That's it," Willie said. "I figure it means he'll only come back as a schmuck, same as he is now."

"Or a conch, the kind that lives in the ocean," said Angel. He looked at Lenny and said, "Youse already got the toenail for it."

———————

It might have been that same day, or maybe another. Events become blurred in paradise. Willie inserted a fresh cigar in his mouth and waved his empty glass at Angel. I sat to one side of him, Lenny on the other. It was late afternoon. Willie lit the cigar and looked thoughtfully at the ceiling. "I got a joke to tell," he said. "Did youse ever hear the one about two guys standing in front of the urinals at LaGuardia?"

"Many times," said Angel, pouring scotch over ice.

"I don't think so," Lenny said, "or if I did I can't remember it."

Willie said, "Well, listen up. We gotta lot ahead of

us before this day is over, and it ain't gonna happen quick. We need to slide into the rest of today and enjoy it. Me and Lenny come out a coupla hunnert ahead from the third race at Belmont, so life is good. First comes the joke, then happy hour arrives, which needs our full attention. After that it's time we found a decent Italian restaurant on this fucking island, which we ain't done so far in how many years? Arnold got a lead on a new one we're gonna try tonight. He says it's Sicilian and just opened, but we'll know right away by the marinara sauce. Then it's back here to the bar till closing. It's a heavy schedule. So, my question is, can youse spare the time?"

"We got the time." It was Lenny speaking.

"What Lenny says is probably true," said Willie, "so here goes wit the joke."

Angel set Willie's drink in front of him and looked at me. "Greaseballs," he said, and shrugged.